OTHER RACES ... OTHER EVILS?

"Adam, you are fighting a battle that has been lost many times in the past. It is the conflict of two cultures —the culture of science against the traditional academic culture . . . the old war between permanence and change.

"That's why I'm afraid of Project Lifeline. I sincerely hope it never picks up any signal out of space, because contact with any higher culture could destroy our world. If you want a parallel, remember what happened to every aboriginal culture here on Earth, when contact with the more progressive European culture brought whiskey and missionaries and diseases."

Adam Cave disagreed. It couldn't be like that between Earth and some unknown civilization Out There. But the result of his persistence was to be different than either debater had thought—tremendously different!

BRIGHT NEW UNIVERSE

by

JACK WILLIAMSON

ACE BOOKS, INC.
1120 Avenue of the Americas
New York, N.Y. 10036

BRIGHT NEW UNIVERSE

Copyright ©, 1967, by Jack Williamson

An Ace Book. All Rights Reserved.

Cover by John Schoenherr.

I

THE BEST OF Earth wasn't good enough. He
was throwing it away, all for the shadowy chance of something better out of space. That was the fact, but the words
were hard to say. Especially to Kayren, because she had
been the best.

She met him at the jetport, with a clinging kiss.

"We're so lucky, Adam. You and I together. Now we've
got absolutely everything!" Her breathless huskiness sent a
tingle down his spine. "It's so good to have you home to
stay."

He wondered uncomfortably how she would take it.

She had rushed straight from a swim at the senator's place
on the lake, her bright curls still dark-streaked with damp-
ness. Scrubbed clean, she was flushed and sweating a little
with excitement now, and her own sweet odor set an ache
of longing for her in his loins.

But he wasn't coming home.

Pink-and-gold with the warm June sun and her own delight, she pushed him back to look at him. He stiffened
against the pain of what he had to say, his lean frame
snapping to attention in the trim black-and-silver as if she
had been an inspecting Space Force general.

5

How could he tell her?

He caught his breath and groped for words and illogically crushed her close to kiss her again. He couldn't bear to break it so bluntly. She had been part of him too long. Their fathers had been pioneers in the project, early leaders of the long search for other life in space. Though he actually recalled neither Dr. Hunter nor his own lost father, he had been in love with Kayren ever since her youthful widowed mother came to work in the senator's Westmark office.

Her lithe, athletic body shivered a little in his arms. He thought for a moment that she had begun to suspect. Herself a business math major, just out of Westmark State, she seemed sometimes to have all her father's bold scientific logic disguised beneath her own child-eyed charm. But then, as she swayed and clung and slipped away again, he knew that the tiny shudder had been only her firmly reined desire.

"I'll bring the car around while you pick up your bags," she said eagerly. "The family's waiting for us, with the red carpet out. The senator is staging what he calls a family shindy for us—"

"Not yet, Kay. Let's— Let's—"

In spite of himself, he kissed her again.

Twenty-two years old, he had just won his jets at the Space Force Academy—on the same day she finished at State. But all his hard training had not prepared him for this crisis. Her melting warmth weakened his knees and his purpose. Yet he couldn't come home, not to stay.

"Let's get a drink somewhere." He clung to her hand, staring down at his diamond on her finger, the huge blue crater stone his father had brought his mother from the moon. "Something—something I must tell you."

"If it can't wait." She nodded gracefully. "But they'll be expecting us. A pretty important affair. Celebrating your jets and my graduation and our wedding. I think your family likes me, Adam."

"I love you, Kay!" His voice came hoarsely, too loud. "You know I love you."

6

"Of course I do," she agreed serenely. "We'll go up to the Planet Lounge for just one drink."

The lounge was dimly lit with glowing models of planets and their moons, decorated with charcoal murals of crater-rippled landscapes. They found a back table.

"The invitations are all addressed." Her bright innocence hurt like a knife. "But your family isn't waiting to be asked. They're all too generous. Your Aunt Victoria is giving us what she calls a rancho home, out in her Spanish Hills addition. General Monk says he'll furnish it. The senator is buying us a car, and the bishop wants to lend us his mountain place for the honeymoon—"

She stopped, leaning across the little table. Her eyes turned dark with sudden fear.

"Your stepfather—" She caught her breath and bravely tried to go on. "He wants to talk to you. Something about a research appointment at the university. Academic status and a fat grant from some foundation—"

Her voice stumbled again.

"What is it, Adam?" The bright sun-color drained out of her face, leaving a few pale freckles. "What's wrong?"

The waitress had come to the table, a plump redhead in black net glittering with tiny silver rockets. His voice harsh and uneven, he ordered two martinis, Kayren's very dry.

"I'm not coming home, Kay." He flinched from her hurt face. "Not to live. So there won't be any wedding. I wrote you the night we got our jets—and tore the letter up. I don't suppose you'll understand. I can't tell you how sorry I am."

The great diamond smoldered on her quivering hand.

"Is there—somebody?"

"Nobody." He grinned bleakly. "There never was anybody else—if that matters now."

She sat looking stunned and bloodless until the redhead brought the drinks. Moving with a sudden start, she caught the burning diamond to strip it off her finger.

"No!" he said. "I'd like you to keep it. If you will."

Mechanically, as if it didn't matter, she slipped it back.

She picked up her glass. It spilled on her quivering fingers. She set it quickly down, untasted.

"Why?" She looked up at his face. "Why?"

"I'm staying in the Space Force."

"But I thought—" She leaned desperately across the little table. "I thought the senator had your discharge all arranged."

"He did." Adam nodded curtly. "But I couldn't go through with his little scheme. Didn't want to, really. Kay, I've volunteered for six years in Project Lifeline. I got the notice yesterday that I've been accepted. I'll be going out to the moon."

"I can't believe it, Adam." Her pale lips stiffened and quivered. "Can you tell me why you're doing this?"

"I'm afraid not, Kay." He shrugged unhappily. "Not so you'll understand."

"Try me." Dilated with pain, her eyes looked almost black. "Is it because your father died on the moon?"

"Maybe." His face twitched. "I guess that's part of it." Fingering the diamond, she waited silently.

"Look at me, Kay." He grinned sickly at himself. "The lucky guy that had everything. Millions—so long as Aunt Victoria doesn't change her will. Family—the family means a lot to me. You—you were best of all, Kay."

"But everything isn't enough."

He sat for a moment watching pain twist her face.

"Sorry, Kay," he muttered. "I just don't know how to make you understand. It's not your fault. Not anybody's. But Commencement night I couldn't sleep—because suddenly I knew that life should be better. Somehow, it ought to offer more than anything we have."

"And the project is your idea of that something more?" She flushed with bright anger. "You're leaving me—you're giving up everything—just to wait on the moon for a signal out of space?"

"I knew you wouldn't understand." Tired lines bit into his face. "But that's our chance of something better, Kay." He tried to smile. "Perhaps the odds aren't so good, but it's the only game in town."

8

"A game that killed your father," she said bitterly. "And broke your mother's heart."

"Don't ignore Joe Runescribe." His strained smile vanished. "I know the odds," he said. "I'm sure my father did. But the promise is worth all the risk."

He leaned toward her, sternly eloquent.

"Think what it would mean!" His eyes flashed with his vast and stubborn elation. "To prove that our fleck of cosmic dust isn't all there is! To learn that we aren't alone! To find other worlds, other minds, other races—older and wiser and more talented than we are! Think of it, Kay. That's what I'm playing for."

She took one careful sip from her martini.

"You didn't tell me." Her voice was dead. "Now you aren't even asking me to wait."

"That wouldn't be fair." He looked up into her level eyes. "I can't make you wait six years—or more likely sixty. It's a bet on planets and creatures and technologies that may not exist in our galaxy. I'm betting my life, but I won't bet yours."

She pushed her glass suddenly away.

"I've lost my taste for extra-dry martinis." She laughed unsteadily. "We'd better go and tell your family now. Get your bags, and I'll bring the car."

She was taking it well, he thought. Even though she didn't begin to understand. Clean and tall and lovely, strong enough for anything, she walked bravely away through his hot haze of tears. Her newest hobby, he recalled, was karate.

His own family failed to take it so well. They were gathered in the old family mansion, which the senator had repurchased and restored as a political gesture. It adjoined an integrated section. A tired Negro was shuffling along outside the high brick wall with a black-lettered placard, MONKS UNFAIR TO MILL WORKERS, and a group of Mexican children stopped playing to stare as a radio signal from the car opened the tall iron gate.

Three generations of Monks and their kind were waiting in the old family fortress, noisy and happy, half of them

9

already tipsy. His mother kissed him damply. The hawk-beaked general shook his hand. Smiling painfully, like a frostbitten cherub, the little bishop escorted him to greet his Aunt Victoria. A wheezing old virgin with a bright scarlet shawl and a thin brown moustache, enthroned on her wheelchair, she presented a seamed leather cheek for him to kiss. The senator's small golden-curled granddaughter dragged them excitedly away to peer into the bedroom piled with the graduation and wedding gifts to be opened after dinner.

The genial senator had been mixing drinks in the glitter of bottles and glasses and ice at his long sideboard, but dinner was already spread in the traditional family style, the great oak table richly burdened with smoking platters and overflowing bowls. The senator himself had grilled the immense tom turkey that lay waiting to be carved, bronzed with hickory smoke and oozing golden juices.

The senator had seated Kayren at his right and Adam at his left. Jovially poised with carving knife and fork, he called upon the bishop to ask a blessing upon the family gathered to welcome this newest and loveliest member—

"Stop it!" Kayren was on her feet before the bishop could begin. "Adam has news for you."

She sat down again, smiling too brightly at him across the great turkey. Her face looked tense and white and her voice had been a little high, but her great blue eyes were innocent and wide, veiling their malice. He felt a spark of admiration for her.

In the startled hush, he rose reluctantly to peer up and down the two rows of waiting faces. Feeling none of Kayren's cool poise, he was choked with a cold regret. He loved these people individually, down to the openmouthed and breathless yellow-haired girl sitting with her grandmother at the foot of that endless table. As a family, they had formed his childhood world, narrow but warmly secure. He hated hurting them.

He drew an unsteady breath.

"The engagement is broken," he announced hoarsely. "It's all my fault. Kayren has been magnificent. I apologize to her, and to all of you. I'm awfully sorry I let things go so far, but—well, I simply didn't see what I had to do, not until graduation night. What I had to do is join Project Lifeline. I'm leaving next week for the search station on the moon." He caught his breath. "All the wedding gifts will be returned."

He sat down abruptly.

"Bravo!" Kayren cooed melodiously over the turkey. "Quite an oration. You should follow your uncle into politics."

"Adam, you're joking!" His mother, beside him, blinked up at him with purple-shadowed eyes. "Aren't you, Adam?"

When she saw that he was not, she suddenly looked too old for her bright makeup. A wounded animal wail came out of her withered, green-painted mouth. She dropped her head into a tiny crash of scattered wine glasses.

The senator growled that he would be damned.

Down the table, Aunt Victoria began writhing and gasping with her asthma. Joseph Runescribe rose to wheel her away. The yellow-haired granddaughter came sobbing from the foot of the table to hug Kayren.

Adam sat flushed and silent, feeling the eyes of all the family on him, shocked and flatly hostile. He wanted to explain what Project Lifeline meant to him, but he knew that they would never understand. He was almost ready to retreat, when Joseph Runescribe rolled his aunt back to her place and the senator called again for the bishop's blessing.

A shrunken, shaven Santa Claus, with his fat red cheeks and fat potbelly, Bishop Monk prayed very pointedly for those pitiful misled souls who dared to doubt that mankind was the dearest creation and the most holy image of God. With a special quaver in his voice, he begged mercy in Christ's name for those fools who sought truth and light and the life everlasting not in divine revelation but out in the wilderness of space.

The senator carved the turkey, distributing white meat and dark with his usual fluent felicity. He rang for his Negro man to pour the wine and proposed separate toasts, one to Kayren and another, ambiguously, to "Adam's better judgment."

11

Tasting nothing, his mother sat crying silently, two broad streaks of purple washing down her withered cheeks and blurring the green around her mouth. Kayren attacked her plate with an air of cool disdain, but he thought she looked secretly ill.

The senator ate with gusto, after the plates were served, and began to question him with an air of Olympian detachment, as if he had been a reluctant witness before some routine committee investigating something no more important than world peace or a new pad for the Westmark jetport.

"Young man," his mellow voice boomed above the clatter of the meal. "I do regret that you failed to consult me before you took this injudicious step. Frankly, I'm afraid you're in for a very painful surprise. I'm afraid you'll find very little support, either political or financial, for any continued American commitment to Project Lifeline."

He paused to spear another brown bite of turkey.

"What leads you to believe in the project?"

Adam straightened, eager to defend himself.

"All our arguments were verified by Kayren's father, while he was project mathematician." He grinned at her dove-eyed innocence. "Every normal sun-type star has its family of planets. One or two of each family must resemble Earth. Carbon-based life appears on an Earth-type planet just as normally as its seas do, with no special creation required."

He glanced uncomfortably at the bleak-faced bishop.

"Evolution guarantees the rise of intelligence, wherever life appears. Natural selection keeps refining mind, which is the ultimate adaptation for survival. The process is automatic. The Hunter thesis says that brains appear as inevitable as rainbows do."

He heard the yellow-haired child whispering sharply to her grandmother. Sick inside, he knew he was losing them all. The abstract idea was too vast for most of them—and he saw the flash of malice in Kayren's limpid eyes.

"Thinking creatures are everywhere!" He hurried on, trying hard to be both exact and dramatic. "The Drake equation proved that, years ago. Dr. Hunter made some new assumptions—about the relative age of our sun and the survival of intelligence. He estimated that one star in ten must have worlds at our own level or above us."

"A beautiful oration," Kayren murmured mockingly. "But you all know my poor father died in a lunatic asylum."

He tried to ignore that ironic thrust.

"Think how many stars there are!" He hurried desperately on. "That's the clinching argument. Multiply the smallest possibility by billions enough, and you have a certainty. Dr. Hunter estimated ten billion superior civilizations, just in our own galaxy.

"Look at the meaning of that. If only one planet in those ten billion makes the technological breakthrough to interstellar flight, you'll have the birth of a great transgalactic culture that will spread in time to all of them. And on, perhaps, to other galaxies—"

"What's that?" General Monk barked down the table, briefly impressed. "If we have that many potential enemies in space, we had better see to our own defenses."

"No danger, General," Adam said. "Anyhow, almost none. Dr. Hunter always insisted we needn't fear invasion. Fossils prove that our sort of life has been evolving for several billion years here on Earth without interruption from outside. That seems to mean that the odds are several billion to one against successful invasion in any particular year, including this one—"

"Toot!" the General snorted. "I'll keep my powder dry."

The senator cleared his throat, with the effect of a gavel.

"You're contradicting your main argument," he interrupted shrewdly. "If space is so crowded with all these superior beings, why aren't they already here?"

"A big question." Adam nodded defensively, feeling them all against him. "That's why I'm joining the project—to look for answers to such questions. But at least one answer seems pretty clear."

He spoke down the table, trying to seem confident.

"Astronomical distances are as great as astronomical numbers. On the galactic scale light itself is slow. And the best

13

theoretical rockets have only a tiny fraction of the speed of light. Actual flight between the stars depends on the sort of scientific breakthrough that Dr. Hunter couldn't calculate."

"I'm familiar with the Hunter thesis." The senator's mellow public voice rolled out roundly. "In fact, it took me in, back in the beginning. We've been voting funds for Project Lifeline for more than thirty years. We keep beaming expensive signals toward every star around us. We never get an answer."

"Replies will take time," Adam protested. "An answer from just the nearest star would take eight years, at the very best. But each year brings more stars into our signal range. We simply can't give up now—"

"I'm afraid the taxpayers are getting a little tired of pouring billions of dollars into every rathole on the moon," the senator broke in blandly. "And my constituents keep asking embarrassing questions. Even assuming that the universe is full of super-minds, why should they talk to us?"

He paused for effect.

"What do you say to a fly in your soup?"

Adam tried to ignore Kayren's pleased smile and the snicker from the foot of the table.

"That's a very serious question," he insisted doggedly. "Out on the moon, I hope to find an answer. If we do pick up a signal from space, it will be the great turning point in human history. It will give our lives a meaning."

"My boy, I'm afraid I just don't understand you." The senator shook his flowing silver mane and turned his genial smile on Kayren Hunter. "I can easily recall a time when the love of this glorious American girl would have filled life with meaning enough for me."

In Adam's awkward silence, he heard his Aunt Victoria chiming a spoon against a glass. A heaving mountain of wounded flesh, she clutched the scarlet shawl around her sagging dewlap and snored for her breath.

"Adam Cave, you've broken—my poor old heart," she gasped at him tragically. "I have loved you dearly—for your poor father's sake. But now you've—you've betrayed me—betrayed the family trust—betrayed a lovely young girl."

Kayren gave him a bright sardonic smile across the turkey skeleton, as if she had begun to enjoy her martyrdom.

"I won't tol-tolerate such outrageous behavior—not even from you," Aunt Victoria wheezed laboriously. "If you go off to the moon—listen to me, Adam! I'm cutting you out of my will. Not one share of anything."

Her watery eyes blinked at him.

"Adam—for my poor old sake—give it up!"

He squirmed uncomfortably, a painful lump swelling in his throat. He pitied her, for the more graceful creature she once had been. He felt grateful to her, for many generosities. He loved her yet, in spite of all she was.

"To say I'm sorry does no good," he muttered huskily. "But I am sorry, Auntie. Truly I am." His eyes fell from the cold faces he had loved. "I'm afraid you'll never understand—even if we do make that contact. But I'll be on the moon next week."

Aunt Victoria swelled and purpled and sank into a fresh asthmatic attack. Joseph Runescribe fluttered back to her side. General Monk caught Adam's eye with a beckoning nod toward the senator's library.

The long dim room had a rich smell of old leather and fine tobacco and austere tradition. The general closed the door, inspected the law-laden shelves, and gestured for Adam to sit across from him at the old teak table.

"What is it, sir—"

Lifting a lean forefinger to silence him, the general took a small disk-shaped device out of his pocket and set it on the table. Adam caught a faint but painful humming from it, almost too shrill to be heard.

"The senator says he keeps the place debugged, but I don't like chances." The general nodded grimly at the thin black disk. "Ultrasonic. Supposed to kill any bug in fifty feet."

Adam waited, wondering.

Deliberately, General Monk opened a heavy silver humidor and lighted one of the senator's strong cigars. Trimmer and taller than his brothers, he had the aggressive family jaw, with a cruel hooked nose and cold yellow eyes. He sat puffing the black cigar, frowning somberly.

"Nephew, I wish you had talked to me." He lowered his voice and carefully slid the squealing disk to a point precisely between them. "I'm afraid your impulsive behavior has got you into a bad situation."

"How, sir?"

His alert eyes flickered at the door.

"You know that Project Lifeline is a joint undertaking, supported by several powers—"

"That's one reason I like it, sir."

"I don't," the general rapped. "I could have advised you that old Hunter's theory of friendly contact with any other planet is an insane utopian delusion."

Adam moved to protest.

"Listen, nephew." The general gestured sternly with the long cigar. "Don't think I'm uninformed or ill-advised. Our facts come from many sources. They've been evaluated by experts. Professionals agree that any interstellar contact would be the greatest danger our world has ever faced—"

"Sir, I disagree—"

"Boy, you've no right to disagree." The general snapped ash from his cigar. "You don't know enough. We put up with Project Lifeline because it may become a useful listening post, but you'll find no future there."

"My father—"

"Listen, boy." The general leaned closer to the shrilling disk. "If you want to tackle the real problem, I can get you into another outfit—one that is fighting to protect us from contact." His steel eyes narrowed. "What do you say?"

"Huh?" Adam caught a startled breath. "Sir, does this mean that some kind of contact is already happening?"

"No comment."

"Can you tell me more about this outfit?"

"If I do, you're in it." Sarcasm flashed across that brown hawk-face. "Why hesitate?"

"Because I disagree, sir." Adam sat straighter. "If trans-galactic contact is possible at all, I believe it is man's

16

great hope. My father gave his life for the project. I'm willing to give mine."

"You won't get much in return." The general kept his voice down, but it crackled with anger. "Toot, boy! We tolerate the project as a harmless boondoggle, but I can promise you that any real contact will be bitterly resisted by every responsible government on Earth."

Adam gaped blankly.

"Sir, I don't understand—"

"Talk to Joseph," the general gritted. "I'm no theorist." Reaching for the whining disk, he lowered his brittle voice. "Listen, boy. Though I've really said nothing, this meeting is secret. If you let one hint slip, the results could be bad for both of us."

"I won't talk—"

"Don't!" The general stood up, yellow eyes smoldering. "You're a stubborn fool," he grumbled brusquely. "You've let the family down."

He muted his black disk and marched back to the living room. Adam stumbled after him, perplexed and hurt, yet excited by his own unanswered question. Was contact somehow near?

To his relief, the family shindy was breaking up.

Kayren kissed him with a hot vehemence, as if to make him sorry.

"Don't hurry back, Buster," she breathed sweetly. "I won't be waiting."

The senator gave him a bland handclasp, and he rode home with his mother and her husband.

Sobbing quietly in the car, his mother whispered accusingly that he was behaving just like his father. She couldn't stand the agony of that all over again, and now she was getting one of her migraine headaches. At the apartment, she glanced at the hall mirror and saw her smeared mask of purple-and-green and ran wailing away to bed.

Joseph Runescribe followed anxiously to give her a tranquilizer. Feeling empty and shaken, half angry and half ill, Adam went back to his old room. He was standing in the doorway, looking at all his books and models and athletic trophies, thinking of the bare ten kilograms he could take to the moon, carefully ignoring all the photographs of Kayren, when Joseph came wanting to talk.

He felt tired of talk—of useless talk and hopeless emotion. All these people he loved had become opponents, dull and cold and ugly. The senator's turkey was an unpleasant mass in his stomach, and the general's warning festered in his brain. He needed to get out, to hike ten miles out of Westmark on some country road, getting things straight again and making a real farewell on this warm June night to the Earth he knew and loved.

A sharp longing caught him, for the project itself. For the mighty transmitters and supersensitive receivers on the back of the moon, shielded there from Earth. For all the labs and computers buried in the moon. For the hard problems to solve, even for all the failures and delays before the triumph of contact—

But then Joseph himself was a scholar, the professor of classical antiquities at Westmark State. A citizen of the academic world, where mind scorned money, he might understand. Adam followed him hopefully back to the den, where they wouldn't disturb his mother.

"Suppose you *are* right, Adam?"

A dark, alert, bird-like little man, Joseph was trying too hard to be affable. He kept darting about the warm, brown, book-lined room to offer Adam things he didn't want: a glass of Spanish brandy, a cup of auto-expresso, even a tranquilizer.

"Just suppose you did contact superior creatures?" he inquired. "Grant the most favorable—and most unlikely—case. Suppose they receive us as worthy young kinsmen—not as monsters or cattle or vermin. Suppose they welcome us into a great galactic civilization and gladly share their high culture with us?"

He paused, his dark face sardonic.

"Would that improve the human condition?"

"The human condition!" Adam made a face at that pet phrase of Joseph's, because it reeked too much of his mother's miserable self-pity. "I suppose a lot of people feel

18

pretty desperate," he said. "I guess the trouble is just that
we want so much more than life can ever give us. We all
want to be happy and beautiful and noble and immortal.
Life makes us sad and ugly and mean—and then it kills
us. But still I don't like the phrase."

His voice lifted fiercely.

"I'm pretty desperate myself tonight—even though I may
look lucky to everybody else. But I won't cry about the
human condition. I think there are two better things that
we can do about it. We can either accept it with whatever courage and grace we can, or else we can try to
change it. I intend to change it. That's why I'm joining
Project Lifeline. I believe contact with a galactic culture
could change everything—for the better!"

"You're wrong, Adam." Joseph tweaked restlessly at the
neat pointed beard that completed the dark triangle of his
face. "If you'll pardon me, you're a very foolish youth—
about to throw away everything that has made you the most
fortunate man alive."

"I want to aid mankind, "Adam said. "Is that foolish?"

"Your method is," Joseph insisted. "You're confusing symbol and reality. While you debated the senator tonight, I
was thinking that these hypothetical space creatures are
only a symbol for the idea of progress—which was blown
up a century ago."

"I believe in progress," Adam said.

"So do Rotarians—but look at history! The old Greeks
were wiser; they put their Golden Age back in the past.
When Aristophanes wrote *The Birds* he was poking fun at
you and your worlds in the sky. You're as gullible as Swift's
poor Gulliver."

He began pulling thumb-worn books from the shelves.

"Look at the satires on progress. Swift's flying island.
Wells' insects in the moon. Huxley's brave new world, where
the hero hangs himself. Pohl's plague of plenty. This odd
old book about the perfect machines, the humanoids, smothering men with too much perfection. They all make one true
point—the idea of progress is a cruel illusion."

"I won't admit that."

"Because you are ignorant of the past. Actually, Adam you are fighting a battle that has been lost many times in the past. Snow lost to Leavis a few decades ago. A little earlier, Wells lost to Gissing and Matthew Arnold lost to Thomas Huxley."

Bird-like, Joseph pecked out another stack of books.

"Snow called it the conflict of two cultures—the culture of science against the traditional academic culture. But, as Leavis pointed out, Wells and Snow had no culture. Actually, it's the old war between permanence and change. As you grow a little older, Adam, you'll come to realize that the good things of life are the permanent things. Change is always destructive."

Solemnly he blew dust off a book.

"That's why I'm afraid of Project Lifeline. I sincerely hope it never picks up any signal out of space, because contact with any higher culture could destroy our world. If you want a parallel, remember what happened to every aboriginal culture here on Earth, when contact with the more progressive European culture brought whiskey and missionaries and syphilis."

"You're wrong," Adam said. "It won't be like that."

"You're deluded," Joseph answered. "Progress can't cure the human—situation."

But it had to be cured, Adam thought. Human beings deserved something better than what had happened to his mother and to Aunt Victoria. He wanted something better for himself and Kayren Hunter. Even the senator and Joseph himself had earned more than their old world was likely to pay them.

"I believe in progress," he insisted. "I won't be a pessimist."

"Someday you'll realize that pessimism is the wiser path," Joseph protested urbanely. "Occasionally the pessimist gets a happy surprise. But you optimists are always disappointed."

He wanted to carry on the argument, but Adam's head had begun to ache. He knew he couldn't win, because Joseph would be armed with the polished academic answers for every hopeful point that Snow and Wells and old Huxley had made. He begged off and went to bed.

Troubled thoughts of Kayren and the general and Joseph Runescribe disturbed him for a few moments. He turned over and put his mind upon the infinite promise of Project Lifeline and fell promptly asleep.

II

THE CRATER DIAMOND came next morning in a neat special delivery package with a crisp note in Kayren's perfect hand. Of course she couldn't keep the ring—unless he decided to forget his idiocy. The *idiocy* was underlined twice.

He left the diamond for his mother to keep. Her migraine was better, and they had a brief visit in her darkened room. She talked about his father, the tall astronaut who had joined the project on the moon before Adam was born.

"Of course I love Joe." Her voice began to quiver. "He has always been such a perfect dear, and even the bishop says he's another Monk. But I'll never get over your father. He b-b-b-broke my poor heart."

She snuffled into a scented violet tissue.

"Adam, dear, I've always loved you so—because you're all I have of him. Your footsteps sound just like his. Sometimes your voice is his." She drew a sobbing breath. "You c-c-can't do this—to your own poor mother—"

He tried unhappily to explain why he had to go, but she wouldn't listen. Her headache was suddenly worse. He pressed the great diamond into her unresponsive hand, and went out to ask Joseph to bring her another tranquilizer.

Joseph drove him to the port next day, and his own spirits rose with the screaming jet. He didn't even mind skipping meals. The family once had been his life—he could remember feeling a thrill of pride every time he announced that his middle name was Monk. He loved his

21

mother still, for all the old times when she had been strong and beautiful and brave. His heart still hurt for Kayren. But he had left all of them behind.

Deliberately, he forgot the general and his warning. His thoughts were on the future—on the wonder of the moon and the challenge of the project and the dazzling promise of the first contact. The moon catapult itself lifted him on a surge of high elation.

Buried in the granite of Mount Whitney, the catapult was man's most magnificent machine. All the hollowed mountain rang with the bone-tingling song of the motor-generators, lifting in pitch as the million-ton flywheels stored power from the nuclear plants.

He reported empty, as ordered, and weighed in on the loading stage, which was a granite cavern far below sea level, so immense that it made a toy of the tall silver rocket standing under the gun. Waiting in line, he strained his neck peering up to follow the bright leaning lines of the rails toward an infinite point in the gloom and glitter of that enormous core.

"Counting down, sir," a gruff Space Force sergeant barked above the roaring air. "Move up."

A blond Swan checked his orders.

He stripped and left his Earthside gear. Hurrying nurses weighed him, injected him, warned him to empty his bladder. Shivering in the thin elastic ship-suit he stumbled into his thrust seat, already numb. He was hardly aware of the nurse who taped the sensors to his chest and planted the needle in his wrist.

Fighting to keep alert, to savor every second of this space adventure, he set himself a mental problem. Ignore the general. Suppose Earth had to initiate the first cultural contact. Using the best possible rockets—those on the drawing boards for the Pluto probe—how long would a manned craft take to reach the Proxima, the nearest known star?

Dull from the injections, he hardly heard the warning horns, but the ten-G thrust of the catapult crushed him like a road roller. The thirteen seconds dragged into thirteen ages of suffocating weight.

Release hit him like another blow. He knew dimly that the rocket was already boring into the midnight sky above the high Sierra Nevada at three-quarters of a mile a second, but all he felt was the battering vibration from air turbulence and then the rocket thrust, endurable at first but growing worse than the catapult.

Even with the catapult, he thought painfully, they still had to make seven miles a second to get away from Earth. Launching from a space platform, the contact ship could save that. By sacrificing everything, by using the biggest possible stack of rockets to push a one-man, one-ton capsule, you might get away from the sun with a terminal velocity five times that. Neglecting everything, say sixty miles a second—

Vaguely, in the numbness of the drugs, he felt the rockets cut off and fire again, felt free fall and crushing thrust, as the guided boosters separated to spiral back to Earth.

Adrift in crashing silence, after the rockets stopped, he dragged his dull brain to work. The speed of light is just over one hundred and eighty-six thousand miles a second. Say three thousand times the best theoretical velocity of a one-ton capsule—

But in spite of every effort he was going back to sleep. A tingling deadness was creeping along his arm from the needle, and he recalled drowsily that the vital processes of space passengers had to be retarded to save oxygen.

He slept.

Aroused once by the slow choking snore of the man in the opposite seat, he groped for his figures again, but all he found was thirst and cold and a dull nausea. His eyes wouldn't focus and his bladder felt too full and then the needle stung again—

In some other dim gray interval, driving his mind to infinite toil, he did find an answer. But it was wrong. It had to be wrong. He slept and woke and doggedly checked the answer again. It was always wrong.

Thirteen thousand years—

He felt giddily grateful for the warning horns and the abrupt sharp thrusts of the vernier jets. Numbly he knew they must be steering into Tycho Pit—the mile-wide shaft blasted into the moon with nuclear charges, so deep it held gases dense enough to cushion a landing ship, with no need of retro-rockets. The needle clicked and stung. A monstrous blackness battered him.

Then his head was washed clear again, his arms aching from the anti-depressant. He felt weak and dry and ravenous. Moving his body in the straps to test its light and even weight, he knew they were down in Tycho Pit.

Two minutes did his problem now—and that wrong answer was right. Neglecting everything, his ideal one-man capsule would reach Proxima in thirteen thousand years. It would arrive at sixty miles a second, with no fuel to slow it down.

Obviously, it would have no living human pilot. A one-ton machine, he thought, might just possibly be built to work after thirteen thousand years near absolute zero. By swinging close around the star, the probe might even turn back home with no need of fuel to stop and start again. After another thirteen thousand years, it might get back to relay whatever data its instruments had managed to gather on that single comet-like pass—if men were still around to care.

That, he thought, was just about the best that men could hope to do. The meaning seemed plain enough. Earth would not initiate physical contact with any world outside the solar system. If contact came, of the sort the general feared, it would be from some higher culture—one so high that human beings might easily seem monsters or cattle or vermin.

Bitterly, he suspected that the family might have been right. In his first leaden depression, he even worded a lasergram to General Monk. Apologies. Admit mistake. Anxious accept more hopeful assignment.

His stubborn pride kept it unsent.

Meantime, waiting for surface transportation to his post beyond the moon, he loafed about the tunnel city that ringed the pit. Allowed to eat food again, washing the depressants out of his system with strong lunar vodka, he found his spirits rising as his bruises healed.

A pert black Swan manned the transport office where he reported every day. To signalize his break with Kayren, he took her twice to dinner at the club high on the rim of the Pit, where thick crystal ports let them watch the arriving rockets dropping under whirling rotors to the great platforms which hauled them out through a great black arch to the Earth gun. She had almost agreed to let him show her how to cook an Earthside steak at her apartment, when he met the stranger.

He was waiting on a bench outside the hotel centrifuge when the man sat down beside him: A rangy, handsome man in a baggy white sweat suit stenciled Tycho Hilton.

"Adam Cave?" His voice was deep and easy and pleasing. "I'm Jason Caine."

He began talking easily about himself—without saying how he knew Adam's name. His father had been a small-town carpenter. He had worked as carpenter's helper to pay his way through the engineering school at Westmark State. He had known the Monks. The huntbrinks kept him informed about the senator, but he was eager for news about the bishop and the Monk girl who had married an astronaut.

Adam studied his vivid, optimistic face. Lazily athletic, with shrewd blue eyes and wavy yellow hair, he looked too youthful to have known Mary Monk before she married the astronaut.

Adam wondered for an instant if he might belong to the general's secret "outfit" that was guarding Earth from contact. But his ruddy face looked too warm and bright and innocent for that.

"The girl's my mother," he said. "My stepfather's a prof at Westmark State."

"What became of the astronaut?"

Their turn had come. The stranger followed him into the sweaty steam of the centrifuge. They vaulted to the saddles and began pedaling side by side. Still weak from the flight, Adam was soon puffing.

"An hour of this every day, with a two-G peak, and

the moon is the fabulous fountain of youth." The stranger was breathing easily. "What about the astronaut?"

"My father made three trips out here," Adam told him. "Working with Project Lifeline. You know the first station was in orbit around the moon—the surface plant came later. My father and a man named Tom Jett were in the station when the South African Peace Action cut off traffic to the moon—nearly twenty-three years ago.

"They could have been evacuated, but the project had been running nine years then, with signals beamed toward Alpha and Proxima Centauri. My father wanted to stay and monitor them. They stayed—and the station crashed behind the moon."

"What could make a station crash?"

"Nobody knows." The dial showed nearly one G and Adam was sweating now, pumping hard to keep even. "There was talk of sabotage, but the project wasn't hurting the Pan-Africans. It was almost a year before Dr. Hunter got a surface vehicle to where the wreckage fell. He didn't find much. A few battered fragments. Not a trace of the bodies."

"In spite of all that, you want to join the project?"

"Because of it, maybe." Driving harder, Adam felt a pang of unease. He hadn't spoken of his own plans. He wondered uneasily what Caine was up to. Anyhow, he had spilled no secrets. All he had said was in the history books. He added soberly, "I hope to carry on my father's work."

"Let's coast a bit." Flexing his long limbs gracefully, Caine didn't seem winded at all, but Adam welcomed the relief. "I want to talk to you about a better proposition."

Caine leaned across the handlebars to hand him a plastic card printed in letters of glowing gold:

LIFE UNLIMITED
J. Caine   Manager

"Of course your project aims to aid mankind." His red smile flashed. "I've no quarrel with that intention—except that it's built on the hope of something for nothing. The

26

project is waiting for pie from the sky. It has been waiting for nearly forty years."

"Interstellar signals take a lot of time—"

"But you won't have to wait, in my organization." Caine nodded at the card. "We're running our own little do-it-yourself program for progress right here on the moon—with plans for a branch on Earth. I think you'd be happier with us."

Adam waited, still breathing hard.

"We control a few useful patents and processes," Caine explained. "We design projects that human beings can do—without waiting for any sort of subsidies from space. The Pit was our idea—we sold it to the actual engineers. Our alloy in the new monorail system doesn't get brittle and break at night. We hold patent rights on a new ice-finding device. We're working now on an atomic process to reduce common moon-rocks to magnesium alloys and crystal quartz and free oxygen."

He paused hopefully.

"Does this sort of thing appeal to you?"

It did. Adam felt a flutter of excitement before he had time to reflect that Caine was an utter stranger, whose artful glibness ought to be mistrusted.

"Think it over." Caine was pedaling faster again. "Talk to my bankers."

Working hard, Adam thought it over. The steamy room tilted and spun. Sweat trickled down his flanks, and his body sagged against the safety-straps. The meter inched up to two point zero.

Caine was somehow more appealing than Aunt Victoria or General Monk. His glowing optimism was a refreshing antidote to Joseph Runescribe's urbane gloom. Adam felt tempted to talk to his bankers.

"Take your time," Caine urged, when they were coasting again. "We're just arranging to open a Tycho office. I'll bring you in to meet the staff and look over the displays. We'll talk about terms. I like your appearance. We can be generous—"

"I'll have to say no." Adam spoke abruptly, half on impulse. "Your offer is exciting, but you have just warned me not to expect something for nothing."

Caine's red mouth made a smiling quirk.

"I'm already committed to the project for a six-year hitch," Adam added seriously. "Anyhow, I do believe in the project. Perhaps it will give us a chance to trade something for something!"

They worked hard again, pushing the meter to two point five, until Caine stopped abruptly, kneading his shoulder.

"Cramp in my arm," he puffed. "Don't know why. But I've had enough."

They went down to the showers. Caine came out of his stall in a light-blue moon-suit as bright as his eyes and his yellow hair. "Good luck with contact." Caine smiled. "But please take this."

He offered a silvery coin, which had a cratered full moon for one face and an almond-eyed Freedom on the other. Adam accepted it, somewhat perplexed.

"A hongkong piece," Caine said. "A rather rare relic of the People's Moon Republic—most of them were melted down for the platinum. But the coin is just a case for one of our devices. Let me show you."

He took it back to demonstrate.

"Twist one face against the other—like this—till you hear a click. Then use it like a phone. Speak to Freedom." He returned the coin. "If this contact doesn't work out the way you hope—if you ever need help of any sort—please call me, Adam."

"Thanks."

More troubled than grateful, Adam stood watching Caine's lean bright figure flowing down the tunnel with the effortless grace of a veteran moonman. He tossed the heavy little coin from his palm and waited, frowning, for its slow fall.

An uneasy impulse told him to drop it down the disposal chute behind him. If it was really more than a coin, he thought, it might easily be a bug of the sort the general feared, planted to eavesdrop on him and all around him.

Yet you had to trust somebody. In spite of all the bright

and easy glibness he somehow trusted Jason Caine more than any of the Monks. Oddly happy with himself, he slid the coin into his pocket and swaggered away toward the transportation office.

The swagger was unsuccessful. Lacking Caine's easy art, he grazed the tunnel wall, rebounded around a corner, and collided with a startled girl as almond-eyed as the Freedom on the hongkong coin. Clawing at the air, he came down all over her shapely white moon-suit.

He tried to pick her up, too vigorously; and sent her flying toward the tunnel arch. Twice humiliated, he shrank against the wall while she settled back with Caine's graceful ease. He deserved anger, but she was laughing at him.

"You Lieutenant Cave?" She had seen his shoulder-patch. "Looking for you—not your karate attack!"

She sang her syllables with an oddly charming accent. Her heart-shaped face was exotic and alluring. Tall for an Asian, she looked like a showgirl but wore the project patch on her skintight suit.

"Am Polly Ming," she said. "Like you, en route to Lifeline."

Though she looked no older than the black Swan, it developed that she held advanced degrees from the Peking and Capetown universities, with additional graduate work at Moscow and MIT.

"No friend of project," she added. "Am what you call investigator. My instructions to determine whether success probable, or people's money wasted." She glanced at her time-ring. "One hour we depart."

The project car, he gathered, had been held for her. He just had time to grab his bag and call the Swan. Seated next to her in the crowded car, he tried to make her see the shining hope of transgalactic contact.

"Project very expensive for people's republics," she informed him firmly. "Our hongkongs needed back on Earth. Workers, peasants die of hunger. We eat transgalactic signals?" Her quick sardonic smile was still bewitching. "Or will your nation pay greater share?"

"Not very likely," Adam said. "You know the project

was American in the first place, but the Pan-Africans accused us of using the old circumlunar station to communicate with spies on Earth. When it crashed, we thought it had been sabotaged—"

"Not so!" she protested sharply. "Not by people's republics."

"Maybe not." He shrugged. "Hunter found no evidence. But that's one reason most Americans have never been enthusiastic about the new joint project." He grinned bleakly, thinking of the senator and the general. "I'm afraid our participation won't be increased."

"In which case, project probably dead."

"You can't kill it!" Adam protested desperately. "I'm not like most Americans. I see the project as our greatest step toward a truly united world. One where workers and peasants need not starve—"

"Am what you call expert." She was enchantingly grave. "Know pro. Know con. Earth waiting two billion years for contact. Don't hold breath for it. Now please excuse. Homework to do."

With a piquant smile, she turned from him and began dictating into a tiny recorder. Her sung tones were strange to him, and he considered her hair. In spite of all those perishing peasants, she clearly patronized an expensive beauty salon. Sleek and straight and black, her hair flowed with glowing rainbows where light struck it.

She seemed as crisply cool to his admiration as she was to the project itself. He looked out at the barren grandeur of the midnight moon. Auto-operated, the sealed car skimmed gravel flats and jumped crater pits. Now and then he saw the track ahead, a bright wire glinting in the full Earthlight.

Polly Ming finished her dictation and stowed her recorder away. He offered to let her look at his map, but she knew the route. He observed hopefully that the project should be given another forty years to justify itself.

"Am sleeping now."

He tried to help her recline the seat, but she did it deftly herself. She leaned back and closed her eyes as if he had not existed. He studied the Earthlit moon again, and began listening to his fellow passengers.

They were mostly miners or construction men in work gear, on their way to a new ice-strike around the moon where the Earth never rose. He smiled at two brown little Cubans, as excited as he was, who were preparing to take movies from the car as it overtook the sunset, and spoke to the miner across the aisle, a stooped and grizzled foreman with a red, merry, Irish face.

"Aren't night runs risky? Don't the rails get too cold here?"

"Caine alloy," the foreman grunted. "Stands cold."

"Haven't I heard of Caine?" Adam concealed his surprise. "Didn't he claim he'd invented an ice locator?"

"Sure did." The miner slapped a brown plastic case on the seat beside him. "Model B, right here. Ice sublimes. Moon-rock's porous. Vapor escapes. Caine invented a water vapor detector. Smells ice under a thousand-meter overlay. How we made the strike. Caine gets royalties. Musta made him millions."

Adam felt the hongkong in his pocket and settled thoughtfully back. They overtook the sun. The car stopped to let the other passengers slide down a fabric chute into a gray waste broken only by one swollen orange-colored pressure tent and the bright metal thread stretching across the dark moon-rock toward the black horizon and the new ice strike.

The car skimmed on. The overtaken sun climbed slowly in the black west ahead, slashing the dead moonscape with cruel fingers of fire and shadow. Polly Ming slept, cuddled in her seat like a sleek white kitten. Adam darted from window to window, studying the moon and his map.

Two long mountains loomed ahead, black as space but tipped with sunlight. The track zigzagged into the narrow pass between them, through a wild jungle of splashed and frozen stone. He found the line of ink-filled pits curving across the south boulder-slope, and checked the red cross on his map.

There it was! The falling station had broken up against the crest of that south ring-mountain, to scatter its tragic fragments far across the plain inside. A dull ache in his throat, he watched the dead moonscape wheel beside the skimming car.

Once he turned impulsively to wake Polly Ming. He wanted to tell somebody that his father and Captain Jett had died on that naked ridge, for the hope of transgalactic contact. But she was no friend of the project. He let her sleep.

Half an hour beyond, the track lifted over another great apron of tormented stone, dived through a canyon a meteor had cut, and spiraled down inside the lofty ring-wall.

Here at last was Project Lifeline! Eagerly he rubbed condensation from the little windows to get a better view of the installations clustered around the blunt black peak that broke the crater floor. With a throb in his throat, he recognized the famous thousand-meter dish. The great antenna was tilted toward the dark north sky, perhaps beaming a signal to Tau Ceti.

Elated, he called Polly Ming.

"Was sleeping." She sat up sulkily, liquidly seductive in the tight white suit. "Have eight more minutes."

"Don't you want to see the big dish?"

"Not impressive." She shrugged bewitchingly, glancing at the window. "On cosmic scale, very little dish." Seeing his hurt, she gave him a faint ivory smile. "Am ungracious. Please forgive."

"I was excited," he said. "I thought you would be."

"On cosmic scale, moon is breadcrumb." She yawned sleepily. "Men are microbes. You hear voice of microbe calling from breadcrumb? If you hear, how answer? Maybe squirt of antiseptic?"

She leaned back and closed her eyes.

Adam sat staring down at the big dish again, all his bright elation crumbling. Miles below and miles away, a silver gleam against the gray gravel plain and the black loom of the terraced cliffs beyond, the great voice of searching mankind had suddenly become a futile toy.

III

THE CAR STOPPED in an airlock tunneled into the central peak. Graceful as a white kitten in slow motion, Polly Ming floated down to meet a group of project officials. Their solemn smiles failed to hide a tense unease. Project Director Kalinin greeted her in ceremonious but halting Chinese. She replied in fluent Russian. The committee escorted her out of the tunnel.

Left alone with his ten-kilogram bag, Adam walked up and down the platform. He read a sign that said No SMOKING in six languages, and inspected yellow-patched cracks in the glassy air-sealant sprayed on the drill-marked walls. Here, at the end of his youth and his affair with Kayren and a long quarter-million miles of space—here was Project Lifeline.

He felt like crying.

A horn squalled behind him. A bulky vehicle catapulted out of a gloomy cross-tunnel, screamed around him on skidding plastic tracks, and lurched to a stop beside the car. A gangling corporal climbed out of the bullet-shaped cab and began loading craters that had been dumped out of the monorail car.

Adam walked up to him. He wore US Space Force insignia on his oil-stained coveralls. His spiky red beard needed shaving. He looked up with green-glass eyes at Adam's silver bar, and did not salute.

"Spaceman," Adam said, "I'm reporting for duty here. Can you help me find the American detachment?"

"You and I are the American detachment." The tall corporal tossed a crate into the vehicle and shook hands with him. "Since the major was recalled. Lend a hand with this crap, and I'll take you down."

Adam hesitated a fractional second, and helped load the vehicle. It was called a crater-crawler. The corporal was Solomon Smith.

"You're okay, Lieutenant." When the last crate of dehydrated rations was on the crawler, Solomon Smith grinned suddenly with one side of his face, the other side expressionless. "But I'm skinnish sorry for you, sir. You're what I was, five years ago."

They climbed into the crawler. Hunched over the tiller, Smith sent it recklessly down a maze of dark corridors. Adam clutched the straps and tried to look unconcerned.

"What happened to you?"

"Same as everybody." They lurched around a narrow corner. "I came up from the academy, just like you. A qualified computerman. Machine translation specialist. Full of sass and vinegar and wild ideas about contact. But this skinnish hole got me, sir. Like it gets everybody."

"How?"

"Red tape." They skidded down a curving ramp. "Skinnish stupidity. Homesickness, too. Earth's out of sight. You keep yelling at the stars, year after year. Nobody answers and nobody cares."

"I care," Adam said.

"Once I did." Smith made a faint half-grin. "Actually, my first duty here was to restudy the Drake-Hunter fraction. I even published a report on the study."

"So you're *that* Solomon Smith?"

Adam looked at him with a new respect. That fraction expressed the probability that a suitable signal aimed at any star would get an answer. The equations involved such factors as the number of stars with planets, the average age of planets, the likelihood that life would appear on a suitable planet, the probability evolution would create intelligence and intelligence create technology.

"I was that Smith." Hauling at the tiller, he made a wry nod. "The way I calculated the fraction, at least one star in a hundred ought to answer us. Maybe one star in ten. Our signals are already reaching hundreds of stars. The figures say we should be getting answers. Maybe we are."

34

"Huh?"

"How can you tell?" Smith squinted cynically. "We don't know what we're looking for. That means we can't tell the signals from the static—if there are any signals."

They stopped at the mess hall and Adam helped unload dehydrated rations.

"Signals can be filtered out of noise," Adam protested. "I've had communication theory—"

"Our theory." Smith's lazy nasal drawl interrupted him. "Not their theory. We keep assuming that the galactic culture is made of beings just like us. Actually, men are too improbable to be duplicated anywhere. Our galactic friends are certain to be different. They may think a million words a second, or one word a year."

They were plunging down a gloomy tunnel.

"You know the hairy theory, but I've been there," Smith was droning. "Second year, I got promoted to data processing. The signals section sends you taped noise to analyze. You encode it and run it through the computers. You try every possible device to filter the static out. Then you look for information—for some sort of arbitrary intelligent structure—in the other noise you have left."

"And never find it?"

"You never know. If anything gets through all your electronic and mathematical and logical filters, you assume that it might be a message. You amplify it and beam it back as your most logical reply. Then you wait another twenty years for an answer."

Savagely, he tramped on the squealing brakes.

"Runs you hairy!" he muttered. "I cracked up a year ago. Got busted down for drinking on duty and insubordination to Kalinin. Now I'm just sweating out the Earth rocket and the chance to go human again.

"Here's our skinnish quarters."

He showed Adam to a bare little niche in a gray-sealed tunnel, and hospitably offered him a drink of the raw vodka which it appeared he was distilling in the crawler shop from sugar and dehydrated potatoes intended for the mess

35

hall. Adam choked down a burning gulp of it, with a bleak resolution not to become another Solomon Smith.

Though Smith snickered at his haste, Adam reported at once to the director's office. The receiving machine took his name and told him to come back in four hours. When he came back, the machine clicked and hummed and finally informed him that General Kalinin was not available.

Next morning it did let him in.

A glass-walled box on the end of the desk held a cubic foot of earth and a colony of ants. General Kalinin sat very straight, staring at the insects. He was a stern lean man with short gray hair and a hard gray face. Adam stopped before the desk, with his crispest salute.

"Lieutenant Cave. US Space Force detachment. Reporting for duty, sir."

"Cave?" Kalinin's cold gray eyes looked up blankly. Ignoring the salute, he left Adam standing at attention. His too-accurate English had a harsh accent. "Your orders will be posted."

"A great moment for me, sir." Adam's voice shook with eagerness. "I've come a long way for this. What will my duty be, sir?"

"Nothing important." Kalinin blinked abstractedly back at the ants. "The Chinese and South African contingents are returning to Earth with Dr. Ming. The project is now on a standby basis, as a result of her inspection. In fact, it is kaput. Unless new support is found."

"Oh, I'm sorry." Adam tried to gulp down a sick feeling that he had thrown away Kayren and Aunt Victoria's millions and his own career, all for nothing. "This is a bitter disappointment to me."

"What do you think it is to me?" Anger flashed in Kalinin's cold eyes. "Lieutenant, I am not a military man. Nor a commissar. I am a scientist. I have given twenty years of my life to the project. To me it has been the hope of a high knowledge that men can never find on Earth. Dr. Ming has killed that hope."

Adam pulled himself desperately erect.

"Sir, can't we do—anything?"

"At ease, Lieutenant." The gray man gave him a worn, bitter smile. "Once I had youth. I was sure. I gladly attempted—anything."

Sadly grave, he shook his head.

"But the years have gone," he muttered. "The bright young men. The clever new ideas. The costly installations. We have tried everything. Everything has failed."

"Why, sir?"

"I ask myself that question when I should be sleeping." Kalinin's gray lips tightened. "I have not the answer. Perhaps we ask the wrong question."

Wondering, Adam glanced at the ants in their glass box.

"I keep these displays to help define the difficulty of our mission." Heavily, Kalinin gestured toward a wide slab of black stone mortared into the gray-sprayed tunnel wall behind him. "The famous Rosetta stone, in plastic replica. With parallel inscriptions in known Greek and unknown Egyptian, it was Champollion's key to the hieroglyphics." A tired frown etched his lean gray face. "If we ever do intercept signals from other worlds, where is our Rosetta stone?"

"Mathematics?"

"Do we know that mathematics is a universal language?" Kalinin shook his head. "Might not another culture be as blind to its glories as my ants are to the light of the sun?"

Gloomily, he studied the hurrying ants.

"Lieutenant, our symbols—words, gestures, tones of voice —have meaning only because they refer to common experience. Though mine is Russian and yours American, we have enough in common to serve as our own Rosetta stone. The carvers of the hieroglyphs were also men. But consider these ants."

Adam glanced at them obediently.

"Our kinsmen," Kalinin said. "They share our own evolutionary origins. They share our experience of survival on a common planet. Their species is ancient and successful. Their social organization is relatively elaborate. If we have

37

no Rosetta stone for them—how can we hope to understand the creatures of another evolution, on another world?"

He sagged moodily forward, staring at the ants.

"The ants have no technology," Adam protested stubbornly. "But any race that picks up our signal will have technology that ought to work as a sort of Rosetta stone—a common experience with the same chemical elements and the same laws of physics in the same universe. That ought to be enough—"

"I hoped so—once." The gray man straightened, stern again. "I'm gloomy today." His cold eyes lifted. "Lieutenant, you will forget what I have said. Your orders will be posted. You may go."

"Yes, sir."

He saluted stiffly and turned unhappily away. Touching the hard bulge of the hongkong in his pocket, he wondered bitterly if it could really reach Jason Caine. A more urgent idea checked him.

"General, please!" He turned quickly back. "May I make one request?"

Kalinin looked up blankly.

"If I have no other duty, sir," he blurted, "could I arrange to see the spot where the old project station fell?"

Kalinin frowned, forgetting the ants.

"My father was on that station." Adam hurried, trying to give him no time to say no. "There are questions about the crash that Dr. Hunter's report failed to answer. I want very much to examine the wreckage myself."

Kalinin's gray eyes studied him without sympathy.

"What caused the crash?" Adam insisted. "The crew had been in contact with a surface base on every pass around the moon. They'd reported no trouble. There's no atmosphere to make an orbit decay."

"Hunter suggests that a meteor hit the station."

"But what became of the bodies?" Adam demanded. "Hunter found wreckage enough to account for most of the station, but not a trace of my father or Captain Jett. Doesn't that seem odd?"

"Hunter suggests that the impact vaporized the crew compartment."

Adam drew a long, anxious breath.

"Sir, will you please—"

"*Nyet!*" Kalinin rapped. "Request refused."

"Sir," Adam insisted doggedly, "have you considered the possibility that the failure of that first station might be related to the failure of the second—"

"I know the Hunter report," Kalinin snapped. "Hunter was thorough. His report closed the case. Dr. Ming would not approve the expense of a new investigation. Even if it could be justified, surface expeditions on the moon are not for raw recruits. You are dismissed, Lieutenant Cave."

The machine opened the door. Wandering back through the gray corridors toward his quarters, Adam felt as old and hopeless as Kalinin. He was weighing the platinum hongkong uncertainly on his palm when the crater-crawler came to a screeching halt beside him. Solomon Smith opened the cab.

"Going somewhere?"

"I hope so." He climbed into the cab, and Smith drove on. "What's your operating range?" A sudden rebel impulse shaped the question. "Outside, I mean."

"Depends on the area." Smith's green eyes glittered with shrewd speculation. "What the skin you got in mind?"

"I want to see the crater where my father crashed." Adam told how Kalinin had refused his request.

"Never knew my dad," he finished soberly. "In a way, I guess my life was pretty good without him. I had my mother and her family. My stepfather's decent enough. But I always missed my dad. Felt I owed him something, for all he lost for the project. Half the reason I volunteered. I want to know what really happened to him."

Smith braked the crawler to a lurching stop in an empty corridor. He sat for half a minute staring across the tiller at Adam. A sudden half-grin lit his face.

"Wanta take a hairy chance?" he asked. "Getting busted? Skinning up your main chance here?"

Adam hesitated. He could smell a faint reek of Smith's

illicit vodka, and he recalled Kalinin's warning about surface expeditions on the moon. But he caught a quick breath.

"I'd take any chance."

"I'll fix it up." Smith slipped the crawler into gear. "Just happens your trip fits into a scheme of my own. I need a helper. If you really want to go, let's shake."

They shook.

Smith fixed it up while Adam was exercising in the project centrifuge. Prudently, he didn't ask all the details. Smith said something had broken the laser link to Earth. He was ordered out in the crawler to inspect the relay towers. Adam was assigned to duty as his helper.

The sealed crawler rolled out of the airlock and across the shadow of the big dish. Adam twisted in his seat to stare back at it, a pang of loss aching in his throat. The dish had held his most splendid dreams. But something now—a vast senseless conspiracy of the whole Monk family and Polly Ming and the unknown vastness of the universe itself—something had spilled all his dreams.

"Gotta push it," Smith grunted. "Not two days till sundown here. Less at the site. You don't have much daylight left."

They followed a cleat-scarred trail across the flat brownish crater floor, toward the dark night marching out of the east. The long shadow of the crawler probed ahead, thrust like a spear toward the dull glare of the terraced east cliffs. At the summit, Smith merely shrugged at the laser tower.

"Trouble farther on," he muttered.

They dropped from hot light into darkness, lurching down the boulder-cluttered outer slope. Far below, when they had come back to sunlight and a smoother surface, Smith stopped the crawler and gave Adam the tiller.

"You're the driver now."

He climbed into the bunk behind the seat and took a long pull from a plastic pickle-bottle of his vodka and went to sleep. Hour after hour, while he snored, Adam drove on.

Across gray flats where every pebble pointed its needle of shadow at the black east. Around ink-pooled craters.

Over the jutting scars and gaping cracks of old moon-quakes.

He left the track between the towers, paused to check his map, climbed the ugly slope of the crater where the station fell. At last, with Smith still gasping and gargling behind the seat, he stopped on the crest.

He knew the crater, from Hunter's photographs: A gray-brown step-walled plain so vast he could see it bulging with the roundness of the moon. The ragged shadow of the rim where he stood already lay nearly half across it, but the trail of debris that Hunter had charted should still be in daylight.

Almost as reckless as Smith, he sent the crawler skidding down the dark, shelving, inner slope. Only a few secondary craters slowed his way across the flat, gray-silter floor. In another hour he found Hunter's trail, every cleat-mark still sharp after more than twenty years.

The skidding descent had jolted Smith half awake. He gulped a pick-me-up from his pickle bottle and climbed down to take the tiller while Adam watched for wreckage.

The fragments had left their own faint trail of black crater-lets, linked now by the inky tracks of Hunter's vehicle. They followed that trail back northward, toward the point where the falling station must have grazed the crater rim.

Awkward in his just-issued spacesuit, Adam rode outside on the platform behind the cab. At each impact point, he swung clumsily down to examine and photograph the twisted metal masses and the wounds they had dug in the granular moonfall.

"One negative clue."

Clinging outside the jolting cab between stops, he recorded terse reports on the crawler's audio system.

"No marks of blast or extreme heat. Sheet metal torn and crumpled. Heavier spaceframe members snapped or twisted. Plastic shattered. But nothing fused. Paint not even burnt."

"So what?" Smith's voice rasped over the beep of the recorder. "That a clue?"

"Hunter's theory of the wreck calls for collision with a

41

meteor big enough to fuse the crew compartment," he said. "But the fragments here show no more damage than you'd expect from a grazing collision with the rim and the secondary impacts down here."

"So what caused the crash?"

"No hint so far."

They pushed on, racing the inky tide that crept out from the sun-tipped westward rim. Standing as high as he could keep his balance on the lurching cab, he searched the dead gray flat. Again and again, he called for Smith to turn from Hunter's trail to let him explore another black craterlet.

Nothing. Always nothing but another boulder. On the unhealing moon, wounds cut a million years ago looked as new as the scars from the wreckage.

Nothing Hunter hadn't found.

The black fangs of the western ridge ate away the sun. The creeping shadow thickened, lapped around the crawler, slowly drowned them.

"Had enough?" Smith called.

"Not yet."

"Can't see much here."

"But the sun's still on the slope. I want to see where they hit the rim."

Smith grumbled a little about time and fuel and the hairy boulder-slide on the steep north rim. Adam saw the glint of the lifted pickle bottle in the cab. But the crawler lumbered on.

In the flicker of the headlamps and the far glow of the sunlit slopes, they traced Hunter's trail. Adam probed with his battery light into a few more craterlets. They started up the steep north slope, but never reached the rim.

Halfway up, they were back in glaring sunlight when the crawler started a new moonslide. They came skidding and spinning wildly down again, huge rocks bounding around them in deadly slow motion.

"Skin me!" Smith was gasping, when the pitching vehicle came at last to a stop in the dark. "Gotta give it up. No tracks any farther. Hunter musta come around outside the rim—but we've no time for that."

Stubbornly reluctant, Adam stood gazing up that unscalable wall. The boulder-slide lifted out of darkness toward the dull blaze of sun on the endless dark cliffs. High against the black sky, he found the narrow notch he thought the falling station must have cut.

"Coming?"

"Wait!"

The sun's last rays had glinted on something brighter than the shattered rock, high up the slope. Leaving Smith muttering in the cab, he climbed after it, jumping clumsily from boulder to boulder. One dark stone rolled beneath him, went sailing lazily down toward the crawler. Ignoring Smith's sullen muttering, he clambered on to the object.

A battered aluminum can. Triumphantly, he carried it down. Smith had already turned the crawler, and they were jolting back toward the dark crater floor as he shucked off his gloves and helmet and opened the can. Audio tape, on a shattered plastic reel.

Something Hunter hadn't found!

The broken reel jammed in the crawler's intercom system. Fingers trembling, he snapped off the shattered flange and rewound the tape. The speakers thumped and hissed and came to life with a curt official voice:

"*Audio log of Circumlunar Station One, Project Lifeline. Orbit K-3462. Space Major James Cave commanding. Captain Thomas Jett recording. Dish tracking Tau Ceti. Taped signal running.*"

The sound track thudded softly off and on.

"*Entering radio shadow.*" That crisp voice snapped again, across more than twenty years of time. "*Switching dish to receiver. Oscillographs indicate nothing unusual—*"

A series of brief squeals cut off the speaker.

"*Got it, Tom?*" A deeper voice boomed. "*Intermittent radio bursts. Ten point eight-five centimeters. Point of origin near Tau Ceti.*"

Adam gasped for his breath. Suddenly weak, he clutched with sweaty hands at the straps that held him in the jolting seat.

"Hear that?" he whispered hoarsely to Smith. "That second voice must have been Major Cave's. My own father speaking!"

Listening, Smith braked the crawler to a lurching stop.

"Got it." Excitement had quickened Tom Jett's voice. *"All monitors recording. D'you think this is contact?"*

For half a minute the speakers hissed faintly.

"Oscillograph shows signal fading." Tom Jett spoke. *"Signal fading fast—"*

"Source drifting out of focus." The deep, even sound of his father's voice choked him with surging emotion, almost as if he had known it before. *"But we're tracking now. Tracking point source."*

Another hissing pause.

"Signal strong." Jett was tense, breathless. *"Getting stronger."*

"Because it's closer." His father's calm, slow tones had little of Jett's excitement. *"Apparent motion of point source means it's something closer than Tau Ceti."*

"Mankind!" Tom Jett was growing shrill. *"Look at that oscillograph!"*

The tape made a frying sound.

"Wavelength running wild." Even his father's deeper voice had quickened with an echo of Jett's taut urgency. *"Could be a doppler effect. Get off that recorder and help me track it."*

The track thumped twice, off and on.

"Audio log of Circumlunar Station One." Time had passed, enough to let Tom Jett recover his clipped, official tones. *"Completing Orbit K-3462. Unidentified signals washed out in radio interference from Earth. We are now beaming standard geometric code reply toward last observed position of source."*

Another double thud.

"Audio log of Circumlunar Station One. Orbit K-3463. Now entering radio shadow of the moon. Cutting main dish to receiver. Scanning estimated new position of radio source."

Static rattled.

"No luck, Major?"

"Found it!" His father's voice was strained and elated and still oddly half-familiar. *"Now on twenty point seven-eight centimeters. Get what that means? If the shift is really a doppler effect!"*

Jett's voice hesitated. *"I—I don't know, Major."*

"It means the source has been decelerating at a peak of many thousand gravities. If they're transmitting on our own twenty-one centimeter band, which I suspect, it means they were making better than half the speed of light when we first picked them up. It also means they are now nearly here!"

A hoarse, rushing sound must have been Jett's uneven breathing.

"It can mean even more," his father went on. *"We began transmitting toward Tau Ceti about eleven years ago. It's about eleven light-years away. If this visit is a reply to our transmission, our visitors must have come at many times the speed of light.*

"Jett, think of that! It means the transgalactic culture exists. It means somebody was waiting on the planets of Tau Ceti for us to call. It means we have made a friendly contact."

Static fried.

"Mankind, Major!" Jett's slow voice was harsh and strange. *"I hope to hell it's no contact. If it is, I ain't so sure they mean to do us any good—"*

"Anyhow, they're on top of us," His father broke in curtly . *"Get on the radar. Now!"*

For another intolerable time, the sound track hissed. In the motionless crawler, Solomon Smith squirmed at the tiller.

"Ain't it the hairy skin!" he muttered sharply. "Transgalactic contact back when I was still a snotty kid!" He stared glassily at Adam. "But what the skin became of your dad and this Jett?"

Listening, Adam raised his finger.

Static crackled.

"Visual contact!" Jett barked abruptly. *"Coming down at*

one o'clock behind us. Closing fast—and we're a sitting duck. Major, I don't like this. Not a little bit!"

"Keep your hide on, Jett." His father's voice was still cool and deep. *"We've waited and sweated a dozen years for this moment. Can't just say we don't like it now. You can't unlight a match."*

Silence roared.

"Mankind, that thing is big!" A breathless awe stifled Jett's voice. *"Ship—what-you-call-it. Sure ain't a rocket! Means they're a million years ahead of us. I never dared imagine—"*

Jett's dazed voice trailed away.

"Billions of years, quite possibly." His father sounded curiously calm. *"With such craft as this, transgalactic crossings should be possible. I suppose this culture could quite literally be older than our galaxy—"*

"Man!" Jett's frightened yelp interrupted him. *"D'you see that, Major? Some sort of missile! Closing up fast—"*

"Jett, what are you doing?"

"Evasive action, sir."

"You can't evade that, Jett. But I doubt that it's a missile. They wouldn't come all the way from Tau Ceti just to shoot us down—"

Something clanged.

"Mankind!" Jett gasped. *"Hear 'em hit us?"*

"No damage, I think—"

"Listen!"

Something clattered against the hiss of the sound track.

"Man—mankind!" Jett was shrill with hysteria. *"Something inside. They've got inside the station! Right behind you, sir!*

"Ah-h-h-h-h!"

Jett's cry of terror faded into a muted whisper of static. The speakers thudded once, and the tape ran on silently until Adam reached numbly to stop it.

"Skin me!"

Solomon Smith reached under the seat for his pickle bottle. He waved it at Adam, blinked out into the soundless lunar night, and thrust the bottle back unopened.

"What the skin happened?" he gasped thickly. "If our transgalactic neighbors got here twenty years ago, why haven't we heard about it?"

"There has to be a reason." Adam sat staring at the battered aluminum can that had held the table, trying vainly to imagine how it had survived whatever had happened to the station and its crew. "I think the big problem of the project now will be to learn that reason."

"I can make a guess," Smith muttered. "I guess our new friends weren't quite so skinnish friendly as your father hoped!"

Hunching over the tiller, he sent the crawler lumbering suddenly through the starlit dark. Abruptly it struck Adam that Smith's surprise had seemed no more complete than his one-sided grin, that all his reactions to this shattering discovery had been somehow forced and false.

IV

To ADAM'S DISMAY, Solomon Smith laughed at the notion of returning to the project. He confessed that he had sabotaged the laser link and had plundered a storage vault to get spare fuel cells for the expedition.

"So we're deserters!" He waved his pickle bottle. "Outside the crater, we'll steer northeast. Night runs are skinnish dangerous, but we ain't got much choice now. With reasonable luck, we can pick up the monorail track and follow the spur line out to the new ice-strike."

Companionably, he offered the bottle.

"Drink to a new career!" he urged. "Never tried mining, but it can't be worse than promoting transgalactic contact. Brought paint to cover the project markings on the skinnish crawler. Sell it at the settlement—"

"I'm no deserter!" Adam interrupted hotly. "And I think the project will be different now." He nodded at the battered can of audio tape. "I think General Kalinin will overlook everything, when we come back with this—"

"You think wrong." Smith's glassy eyes shone shrewdly. "Kalinin might forgive us for skinning up his laser link, but he won't forgive that hairy tape. You gotta face the facts of contact."

He tipped up his bottle and exhaled fumes of raw vodka.

"The big wheels don't want contact." He blinked owlishly. "Maybe they tolerate the project—as a sort of scientific circus. But any chance of real contact scares 'em skinless."

"I can't believe—"

"The fat cats have already got the world where they want it." Alcoholic cunning narrowed Smith's green eyes. "They can't stand the skinnish risk of any change that might tip over all their goodies. Tell me why they'll welcome contact with any high culture—friendly or not."

"I'm not that cynical," Adam protested. "I'm going back. I think this tape will save the project. I intend to find out what went wrong with that first contact—what happened to my father and Tom Jett. The facts might lead to a real contact."

"You're a hairy idiot—"

"You're drunk," Adam said firmly. "You don't know what you're saying. But we are still in Space uniform. Just now I'm your superior. I order you to take the crawler back—"

"Skin me!" Smith chuckled thickly. "Out here in the craters, rank don't count. But we'll play it fair and squish—mean square." He fumbled clumsily in his uniform and produced a heavy coin that looked to Adam like Jason Caine's hongkong. "Heads we head for the ice-mines, tails we turn back to ol' Kalinin and his hairy ants—"

"You're drunk." Adam shifted cautiously back. "I won't agree—"

But Smith must not have been so drunk as he acted. His angular arm reached to toss the coin and came on with a flashing movement toward Adam's head. Awkward in the pressure suit, Adam tried to duck, but darkness exploded in his brain.

He woke leaning back in the seat behind the tiller, half supported by the stiff suit. His mouth was dry and his cramped body tingled. He found an aching lump back of his ear, where Smith must have hit him.

Smith was gone.

His own helmet lay where it had fallen at his feet. The inner valve of the little lock was sealed, and the outer one stood open to the lunar midnight.

The audio tape—he gasped when he thought of it. Stunned again, he searched the intercom console and then the whole cab. The dented aluminum can was gone.

Every movement hurt his head. Carefully, he drained a few sips of bitter tea left in a hot bottle, and dully tried to think. Smith's departure was hard to understand.

The crawler was stopped on a flat moonplain, still facing west. The panel clock showed seven hours gone, but the high crater wall ahead looked the same. The crawler had not moved far. The monorail track must be fifty miles away by the nearest route, the project base a hundred miles ahead and the ice-mines nearly twice as far behind. Such distances at night were too great for a man without a vehicle.

He snapped on all the crawler's lights and peered groggily outside, hoping to see where and how and why Smith had gone. The gravel-sifted surface was level around him, broken only with random craterlets and a splash of shattered boulders on the right. The black-shadowed cleat-marks of the crawler itself laddered away ahead and behind, but he found nothing else.

No tracks of another vehicle. No skid-marks of a landing ship. Not even bootprints.

Perhaps the gravel here was too firm to show footprints. Perhaps Smith had wandered drunkenly away in his pressure suit—with oxygen and power that would last no more than a dozen hours. Perhaps he was lost out there in the bitter dark, freezing or asphyxiating.

Haunted by that possibility, Adam started the crawler

and drove slowly in a wide circle around the spot, stopping often to look for traces. He found no marks of anything except the crawler itself.

Reluctantly, he gave up the search. The crawler was not supplied to live through the long lunar night. Even in the double-hulled cab, he was already numb with cold. His head throbbed and his eyes ached. Suddenly aware of hunger, he groped hopefully in the cold box. All he found was a nearly empty pickle bottle and a reek of Smith's vodka.

He drove back to their own trail and followed it west, up the shelving wall, back toward the relay towers. Once he stopped to replace a dead fuel cell, and again he woke up stalled in a crater off the trail. A long time later he jolted over the last ridge into view of the clustered lights of the project, miles below on the starlit moonplain.

A tall Congolese corporal let him into the airlock and escorted him to the director's office. Standing gaunt and gray beneath his black copy of the Rosetta stone, General Kalinin scowled across the desk and ignored his tired salute.

"Comrade Spaceman Adam Cave reporting." Kalinin looked sardonically at him, but spoke to a desk recorder that was beeping regularly beside the black-covered box of ants. "Spaceman, you are under investigation. Your words are being recorded as evidence. Now, having been so warned, do you wish to give an account of this escapade?"

"I do, sir."

Reeling with fatigue, he told his story.

"That audio tape can save the project," he finished hopefully. "It proves that interstellar contact is possible—because it has already happened, sir! I think it proves that a friendly transgalactic culture is established on the planets of Tau Ceti—"

"Spaceman," Kalinin interrupted harshly, "I can draw my own conclusions. My first conclusion is that your narrative is a clumsy fabrication—"

"Sir!" Dazed, Adam shook his head. "Why should I lie?"

"One imagines that you hope to escape punishment for the murder of Corporal Solomon Smith."

"No!" Adam gasped. "You can't accuse me—"

"I do accuse you," the stern general snapped. "Smith is missing. You were both absent without leave in a stolen vehicle. You have brought no evidence that this tape exists. Your own account of it is scientifically preposterous."

Adam swayed on his feet, gaping with a dark astonishment.

"Your transgalactic craft!" The general's voice dripped icy contempt. "If it had really come from Tau Ceti in response to our signals, it must have come at several times the speed of light. No competent scientist will say that anything can break the Relativity Barrier."

He leaned abruptly over the beeping recorder.

"What became of Corporal Smith?"

"I don't know." Adam caught an anxious breath. "But we've got to find him. Take me back there in daylight, sir. I can identify the spot from the crawler tracks. If Smith wandered off in the suit, we can surely find him—and the tape!" Sheer desperation shook his voice.

"That audio tape does exist, sir. It reports the fact of contact. The fact is enormously important. To the project. To all the world. You've simply got to believe me, sir!"

"*Nyet!*" Kalinin rapped. "To me your story is nonsense. In my position here, however, I am neither detective nor judge. Frankly, I'm sick of the peculiar antics of your national contingent. I wash my hands of you."

"Sir! May I call my uncle?"

"Impossible." Kalinin's gray lip twitched ironically. "Your compatriot's sabotage of the laser link has not yet been repaired. However, you may see your uncle soon."

Staring frostily at the recorder, Kalinin raised his dusty voice.

"Comrade Spaceman Cave, you will remain under arrest. You will be returned to Earth, by the earliest available transportation. A full transcript of your record here will be forwarded to your own national authorities."

"General, I won't—I can't leave the moon. Not without that audio tape!"

"That is all, Spaceman Cave."

As if he had ceased to exist, the grizzled general stopped the recorder and uncovered the ants. The quiet Congolese escorted Adam out of the room, back to his quarters, up to the monorail station, and all the way to his thrust seat in the rocket at the Tycho catapult, with no time even to call the black Swan.

The flight was a gray nightmare, dripped through the needle in his arm. He stumbled dully out of the rocket at Panamint Field, under Mount Whitney, starving and dehydrated and stinking with his own stale sweat.

Three men met him. A flint-faced Space Police sergeant. A beefy, blue-jowled Space Force major from the staff of General Monk. A slick-haired, sallow-skinned civilian lawyer from the senator's office.

He wanted them to leave him alone. Earth gravity was a dragging thrust that he couldn't stop. He needed a steak and a few drinks and a long night's sleep. They gave him two aspirins and fifteen minutes for a shower at the jetport.

When he came out of the shower stall, wrapped in a towel, they confronted him with the platinum hongkong. The major held the coin as if it had been a snake coiled on his palm. The sergeant had drawn his gun. All three looked pale and shaken.

"Spaceman," the major rasped, "what is this device?"

He stared at it, staggered.

"I don't know." He felt a smoldering anger at them for searching his belongings, and then a quick regret that he hadn't tested the device. But his brain was still clogged with the flight depressants. He couldn't decide what to say. "It—it looks—like a coin."

"Just a mucking coin, huh?" The lead-eyed sergeant pushed the gun closer to his face. "Spaceman, this ain't no funny game. You're in bad trouble now. Where did you get this mucking device?"

"Uh—" He gulped and shook his throbbing head. It was all too complicated—and suddenly he didn't want to talk about Jason Caine. He looked at the lawyer. "Do I have to answer?"

"Not if the answer might incriminate you." The sallow

man leered at him suspiciously. "Matter of fact, I have a message from your uncle. Don't say anything. Play along. Let the family take care of you."

The lawyer turned to the others.

"Therefore—uh—" he muttered sullenly, "therefore I advise my client not to answer any more questions at this time."

The sergeant wanted to put handcuffs on him. He felt too numb and dull to make any protest, but the lawyer halfheartedly intervened.

"He's General Monk's nephew," the major agreed reluctantly. "I'll be responsible."

He put on the Earthside gear the lawyer had brought, and went along with them. He felt too stunned and ill to do anything else. Seated with the silent sergeant on the jet, he tried to clear his head, but all he could remember was his last flight home, just a few strange days ago, when he still had been the lucky young man with absolutely everything.

The senator's quiet Negro chauffeur met them at the jetport and drove them downtown across the river bridge. By that time he felt more alert. Squeezed between the major and the lawyer in the back seat of the ponderous old limousine, he felt a glow of hope when he saw the square gray mass of the Monk building looming through the brown smog in the park. The family had ways to handle everything, if he would only play along.

Outside the basement garage, the lawyer scowled at a sad-faced picket limping under the legend, MONK MILLS UNFAIR TO LABOR. The Space Force sergeant hurried him into the elevator and watched him warily. They got off at the second floor, where the senator's Westmark office overlooked the smog-blighted park. Walking ahead of the sergeant into the huge reception room, he found Kayren Hunter at the desk.

"Have a seat, gentlemen." She looked coolly alluring in a light-blue business suit that accented her honey-colored hair. "The senator will see you in a moment."

The black-clad sergeant shifted his holstered gun and took

a strategic position by the door. The major sat down uncomfortably. With a murmured word to Kayren, the lawyer pushed on through the inner door. Gulping, Adam crossed the deep carpet to the desk.

"Hello, Adam." She smiled up at him demurely. "So sweet of your uncle to let me have Mother's old place here, after you had left me with nothing else to do." She glanced too innocently at the Space Force sergeant. "We weren't expecting you back so soon."

"I haven't come back to stay." He lowered his voice. "You can help me, Kay. You know what happened to me on the moon?"

"We've seen your file."

"Then you know about the audio tape—the actual record of contact with a ship from Tau Ceti. It was stolen from me, under very queer circumstances. I want to get back to the moon and recover the tape and establish the facts—"

"You're in trouble, Adam." A quiver of emotion broke her voice. "Don't you realize that?"

"I didn't kill Solomon Smith," he protested bitterly. "In spite of Kalinin's report, that tape does exist. Kay, I heard my own father speaking. I've got to discover what became of him."

"Remember what happened to my father, Adam." Her eyes turned dark with pain. "He went back to the moon, you know. After he made his report on the crash. To the second project. Mathematician assigned to the American contingent. Stayed four years and came home crazy."

He nodded uncomfortably. "I heard about it."

"His story was a little like your own—"

A light glowed on her phone panel. Already deftly efficient at this new job, she picked up the receiver, listened for an instant, pressed a button. He liked her quick, clean grace. Her show of emotion had touched him. When she leaned to set the receiver back, he caught the perfume of her bright hair. A savage flood of feeling swept him.

He wanted her lithe athletic beauty and all their old friendship, to take and hold and keep. He wanted love and peace and joy. Achingly, he wanted all they might have had together. He wanted everything that came with her, even the approval of the Monks. His throat hurt with longing, and his hot tears blurred her hair.

"Kay!" he breathed desperately. "Dear Kay—"

But when she looked up again she had recovered all her poised control.

"I was telling you about my own father." Her golden tones flowed smoothly on. "When he came back, he'd changed his mind about the crash. He'd somehow convinced himself that your father and Captain Jett were still alive. He kept insisting that he had seen them, spoken to them, on the moon—"

"Huh?" Adam blinked. "I never knew that!"

"It was all hushed up. For sake of his own reputation. Because he had no evidence at all. He couldn't explain why Jett and your father should be hiding on the moon, using other names. His whole story was pure insanity."

"Are you saying— "Adam's voice broke hoarsely. "Are you hinting I'm crazy?"

Her cool blue eyes studied him for half a second.

"You are in trouble, Adam," she said at last. "You must try to realize how serious it is. I think your uncle will advise you to say no more about that tape until you can show some actual proof."

"Kay, you've got to help me!"

He lurched across the sleek desk, bracing himself with both hands against the cruel gravity of Earth. He felt clumsy and slow from the depressants. The long room seemed queerly unreal. Smiling too brightly through his gray mental haze, Kayren herself was now an aloofly beautiful stranger.

"Of course we're going to help," she was cooing smoothly. "Your uncle is calling a family conference to take care of you. But you must forget that tape."

"I'm not crazy!" he whispered hoarsely. "But I don't get this. It's—somehow wrong. It's like a monstrous conspiracy. To kill the project. To stop contact. To prevent progress. To cover up the truth—"

Another light glowed on the desk.

"Of course you aren't crazy," she agreed serenely. "But your uncle is ready now."

The senator came strolling easily out of the inner office, looking very trim and dapper for a man of his weight. He shook hands blandly with Adam, nodded genially to the major, and led the whole group down a corridor to the board room of the family bank.

Following, Adam felt a growing comfort. He knew the old Monk building. A massive cube of steel and stone, it had been a secure family fortress since he was a boy. He remembered coming here with his Aunt Victoria, to play in the hushed and gloomy rooms and corridors while she was at her meetings. Surely the family council would find a way to help him now.

They left the outsiders to wait in the familiar anteroom, though the sergeant seemed obsessed with a sullen suspicion that Adam was looking for a window from which to make his break. Little Joseph Runescribe came darting with a worried haste to meet him at the board room door.

"Your poor mother didn't feel able to come," he whispered. "The shock of your arrest was too much for her. Her migraine again. She asked me to give you her love. Your Aunt Victoria is sitting with her. Call Victoria, Adam! You know she really wants to forgive you."

Nodding blankly, Adam followed the senator into the board room. General Monk and the bishop were already seated. An age-pinched and short-tempered little Santa Claus, the bishop twinkled at him frostily. The general's cold yellow eyes peered watchfully across his little anti-bugging device, which was already shrilling faintly on the great baize table.

"Well, Adam?" With an actor's deliberate ease, the senator sat down at the head of the table. Consciously handsome, he tossed back his flowing hair. "We have all read General Kalinin's report of your unfortunate escapade on the moon. Now I learn that the Space Police have found a spy device on your person. What have you to say for yourself?"

"I didn't know—I don't know that the coin is a spy

56

device." He reeled unsteadily, clutching the back of an empty chair. "It was given to me by a stranger I met in the Tycho Hilton. He wanted me to give up the idea of contact and go to work for him. He said the coin was a sort of phone that I could use to call him."

He shifted his sweaty hands on the chair.

"But I never used it," he said. "I have never given up the hope of contact."

"You're a tooting fool!" The general glared at him, and reached to adjust his shrieking disk. "You'll ruin us all."

"Go on, boy." The senator's urbane voice rose above the louder scream of the disk. "You're still almost a Monk. Tell us all you can in your own defense."

"Thank you, Uncle." He swayed giddily behind the tall chair. "There's a lot I don't understand. Sometimes I feel that the whole world has joined a horrible plot against me. But a few things I do know."

Facing them, he caught a gasping breath.

"I did not kill Solomon Smith. I did find a can of audio tape, recorded by my father and Tom Jett, which tells how an interstellar ship made contact with them. That tape disappeared, along with Smith."

He stopped, desperately watching their faces. The senator's oily, shallow cheer. The little bishop's fat and frigid piety. The gaunt general's restive, hawk-beaked hostility. Joseph's nervous, self-centered concern.

"I want to go back to the moon." In spite of the faces, he plowed doggedly on. "I want to find Solomon Smith and clear my name and recover the tape. With the tape to prove contact is possible, perhaps we can save the project."

Urgently, he spoke to the senator's fixed, political smile.

"The project is falling apart. The Chinese and South Africans just pulled out. I was the last of the American contingent. We've got to go back. We must complete that broken contact my father made. We must find our place in the transgalactic culture—"

"Transgalactic toot!" the general snorted. "Nephew, you're in no position to dream of exploits on the moon. You'd better think of saving your neck right here on Earth."

The senator nodded in bland agreement.

"Perhaps you don't realize the kind of trouble you're in." His fluid voice pealed above the squealing disk. "Unfortunately, the matter is far more serious than any charge of foul play in connection with Corporal Smith. It relates to the contact problem—"

"But, Senator," Adam broke in desperately, "that lost tape proves that contact is possible!"

"Precisely." The senator tossed back his silver hair. "I used to vote my support when Project Lifeline was a harmless symbol of our own scientific progress. But the threat of actual contact with a superior alien culture is something else again. Right, Joseph?"

"Right, Senator," Joseph Runescribe echoed promptly. "It would destroy us as surely as a few Spanish *conquistadores* destroyed the Incas and a few British settlers exterminated the native Tasmanians."

"Understand me, Adam." The senator spoke with a mellow eloquence. "Personally, I don't question your story about that tape. And, if I may say so, I'm a qualified expert."

He bowed smugly to the bishop and the general.

"Unidentified flying objects are my official hobby." He beamed jovially at Adam. "I have checked thousands of reports more circumstantial than your own. I always took them for harmless moonshine. When the voting morons begin to believe them, however, they are not so harmless. True, Joseph?"

Joseph nodded vigorously.

"True, Senator," he eagerly agreed. "Even the rumor of a higher culture could shake our pride in ourselves and shatter our image of our own unique identity and kill all our reason for achievement. Even a false report of transgalactic contact could destroy human culture—if people really believed it."

Adam staggered backward.

"Solomon Smith told me the rulers of the Earth were the enemies of contact." He was hoarse with shock. "I couldn't believe him then—but I begin to see it now."

He stood swaying, blinking at the false public mask of

the bright-maned senator and the fat insolence of the little bishop and the baleful glare of General Monk.

"You would reject any gift," he whispered bitterly, "from any higher culture. No matter how much it would help all humanity. Just because it would lessen you!"

"You phrase it rather harshly." The senator shrugged with an air of smug toleration. "But at least you have begun to grasp the family point of view."

The bishop coughed and shivered, like a little invalid Santa Claus.

"I might suggest prayer." His voice had a high, sweet quaver of inhuman holiness. "But I fear that our dear kinsman has passed beyond the reach of prayer." His tone turned flat and ugly. "Let's get on with our business."

Joseph darted Adam a birdlike look.

"For his poor mother's sake, be generous!"

"Unfortunately, he has left us little choice." The senator swung suavely toward him. "Nephew, I think you have begun to understand that the hazards of contact were recognized by people in important places long ago."

"I understand," Adam muttered wryly.

"Perhaps you don't know that an underground organization has been created to defend mankind from contact—or even from the dangerous faith that mankind can find a secular salvation in the stars."

He made the bishop an ironic little bow.

"I remember—" Adam darted a sudden glance at the hawk-beaked general. "General Monk hinted at something of the sort. I wouldn't believe it then."

"You'll believe it now." The general glared at him with cold yellow eyes. "Because you'll be a member of it."

"That's right, my boy." The senator's voice dripped an oily sympathy. "The organization is named *Man First*. It is international in scope. It controls unlimited resources. And now you must join, because *Man First* allows no outsiders to know of its existence."

Cheerily, he glanced around the table.

"Are we all agreed?"

Folding his fat, pink hands like a toy Santa Claus, the

bishop bowed reverentially. Joseph Runescribe nodded jerkily, like a small dark doll. General Monk extended a quick yellow claw to stop his whining disk.

Adam stared around him frantically. He saw the door beside the fireplace and recalled the executive washroom beyond. He remembered taking refuge in the washroom once, when Aunt Victoria was angry. She couldn't follow him inside, because it was a men's room.

It had a window, he remembered, that opened toward the park.

"Joseph," the senator was booming. "Will you ask the Space people to step inside?"

"Just a second," Adam said. "I've got to use the men's room."

Not too fast, he walked to the washroom door. He heard the general's angry shout, but he didn't hesitate. The door was not locked. He darted past the basins and the stalls to the window. He saw the park across the street. Heat-parched trees, cluttered lawns, jostling crowds—a bright mirage of escape. He saw a mob of largely naked urchins, black and brown and white, screaming in the spray from an open fire hydrant, gloriously free. Down on Grand Avenue, not twenty feet below, he saw three empty taxis standing ready for him at the curb.

But the dustless plastic window wouldn't open. He battered the wide one-way pane with a heavy metal trash-can, but it wouldn't break. When they came after him, they dragged him out, and not even Joseph intervened to keep the handcuffs off his wrists.

V

ADAM WANTED A last word with Kayren, but General Monk shook his hawk-beaked head. In the car he tried to speak to Johnson, the quiet, intelligent, light-skinned Negro who had once studied law and hoped to practice with the senator, but the major raised the glass partition. At the jetport he begged for a sandwich and coffee, or even a drink of water, but the bull-necked sergeant rushed him aboard a sleek little police jet. It shot away at once, with no other passengers.

Sitting chained to the sullen sergeant, he fell into a miserable despair. The state of his body was part of it. He had eaten nothing since the pre-flight routine emptied him on the moon, and his mind was heavy with the depressants still in his blood. He felt vaguely ill from the sergeant's goat-like odor.

But the dark riddle of his own kind hurt him more. Kayren was still stunningly lovely, his longing for her still a haunting pain. The Monks were still decent people, solidly right, his own family and the salt of the Earth; he owed them everything. The Space Force still existed to serve and defend the nation; he still felt the awed devotion of his oath of allegiance.

Yet, somehow, with no justice or reason he really understood, they had all become his enemies. Kayren had sold him out. The Monks had disowned him. The Force had abandoned him.

He sat up in the thrust seat, with a clink of the cold little links. Forget Kayren, he advised himself. Look to the future—if you have a future. Discover the secrets of *Man First*. Learn what happened to your father on the moon. Perhaps you'll see the way to a better world than the Monks can understand.

For a start, find out where you're going.

The little windows were shuttered, but the translucent green blinds were glowing with sunlight on the right-hand side of the cabin. That meant a southerly or easterly heading. Hopefully, he tried a question:

"How far—"

"Don't talk," the sergeant gritted.

He set himself a problem in dead reckoning. Though his watch was gone, along with the platinum hongkong, perhaps he could approximate time and distance. But he needed that cup of coffee. When he yawned and stirred again in the seat, the sergeant jerked sharply at the little chain.

"Muck it, sit still!"

He sat still and watched shutters darken. By now, he guessed, they were over the Mississippi Valley. Still the jet sighed on. Facing away from the sergeant's odor, he thought vaguely of counting seconds to estimate the time, and then he must have dozed.

Where they landed, it was night. Hauling impatiently at the handcuffs, the sergeant hurried him off the jet. His first thought was to look for the moon or the stars, but the sky was overcast. The air felt humidly hot.

The field looked small but busy. Half a dozen military jets stood around them on floodlit pads. A trim Australian fighter was catapulting off. He saw the red Soviet star on a big cargo craft, and the golden Pan-European wheel on a troop transport.

"Keep your eyeballs in," the sergeant snarled at him. "You'll wish you hadn't seen so mucking much."

Lightning flickered in the purple core of a topless cumulonimbus mushrooming overhead, and he caught a blurred glimpse of dark forest walls around the field.

A little car came racing to pick them up, but a sudden gust of cold wind burst ahead of it out of the cloud. He caught a dank whiff of jungle, then the sweetness of rain. Thunder grumbled; great icy drops spattered the pad.

Adam blinked at the driver who jumped out to open the door. A gigantic black, with a handsome, narrow, arrogant face. He wore odd shoes and a creased red cap and a bright yellow loincloth. A queer golden symbol was painted or branded on the sleek black velvet of his upper arm.

Astonished, Adam turned to his guard.

"Don't ask no mucking questions," the sergeant growled. "Just get in the mucking car."

He slid clumsily into the car ahead of the sergeant, wondering dazedly how long he had dozed. Perhaps this was some queer corner of tropical America or even Africa. But white hail was suddenly drumming on the car and bouncing on the pavement. That puzzled him, because hail was uncommon in the tropics.

The terminal building was long and low and new, all bright metal and pastel concrete and shining glass. It looked as clean and commonplace as the senator's new municipal airspace terminal back at Westmark. Looking for a sign that might help him locate it, he saw only the painted emblem over the entrance, cast in massive concrete.

A huge black shield. Bold white block letters across the top, *Man First*. Below the legend, a clenched white fist.

Inside the terminal, he found an air of brisk but relaxed efficiency. Three blonde Swans were eating box lunches in the coffee shop, and a tall Pan-European pilot had stopped to flirt with them. Two Space Force colonels in jet suits were waiting at the flight control counter.

Adam paused to frown at the man behind the counter. Tall and naked and black, he was the driver's identical twin. His lean, high-cheeked face had the same handsome arrogance. His long eyes had the same smoky color. He wore the same tight red cap and the same yellow brand.

"Ain't no mucking rubberneck tour." The sergeant jerked the clicking chain. "Come along."

A quiet electric truck came gliding by them, piled with crated jet freight. Big and black and arrogant as the chauffeur and flight control officer, the truck driver made triplets of them. He called something softly to the man at the counter.

"Don't strain your mucking ears," boomed the bull-throated sergeant. "They don't speak no language of yours."

An elevator dropped them into the antiseptic reek and blinding glare of a medical laboratory. A fourth identical black sat at a key-punch machine beneath the clenched white fist of a *Man First* poster.

"Full name? Date and place of birth?"

The bored sergeant snorted the questions and translated his answers into the clicks and twangs of a language strange to him. The black punched his answers on cards that went to a big computer whirring in the room beyond.

Stripped, he sat shivering on a cold metal stool while other precisely identical black experts took his fingerprints and his photograph and a sample of his blood. Barefoot on the cold tile, wearing only handcuffs and a brief white robe, he shuffled on from test to test, until at last the sergeant unlocked the cuffs and pushed him into a bare gray room.

"Like it or muck it, you're in *Man First* now."

The steel door *thunked* solidly shut. The room was a gray concrete cell, with no feature that offered escape. It was also a comfortable little apartment, he discovered, with a clean bath and a bar that dispensed ice-water and hot coffee and even a box of sandwiches when he punched the buttons.

Grateful for the sergeant's absence, he considered the identical blacks and *Man First*. The blacks perplexed him. The first herculean specimen had taken his breath; half a hundred taxed belief.

Yet he found an ironic satisfaction in all the evidence that *Man First* was actually as powerful and extensive as General Monk had hinted. If the fear of transgalactic contact had stimulated such a response, then the reality must be closer than he had hoped.

He tried to listen as he ate, but the cell was soundproof. He sat down on the white-sheeted bunk to grapple with his problem. Earth's gravity was still a dragging burden. A dull numbness crept over him—

"Spaceman Cavel!"

The brisk male voice roused him from a long nightmare of search for himself. He had been running through endless underground corridors and dashing around corners and peering into mirrors, but the only self he ever found was a naked, golden-branded black man. The black self spoke to him in Kayren's voice, warning him softly not to muck around with *Man First*.

"Spaceman Cavel!" The real voice rapped from a concealed speaker over his bunk. "You will be escorted from your quarters, one hour from now, for an interview with General Masters. Please prepare yourself."

The voice neglected to say who General Masters might be, or how he might prepare himself. He showered, shaved, and punched the bar for juice and coffee. Looking for the scanty white robe he had left in the closet by the door, he found his own clothing, freshly cleaned. His head felt clear again, and he was waiting with a pleasant sense of alert expectation when the gray door swung open.

A tall, gleaming black greeted him with an odd little bow and beckoned silently for him to follow. He followed along the gray concrete corridor, followed into a window-less gray cell that moved away like a horizontal elevator, followed out at last into a sunlit garden.

Looking for geographical clues, he found few. The local time was about noon. The jetport was out of sight, but a sudden shockwave slammed through the steamy air. Low pastel buildings walled a wide court around him, and tall forest made a dark barrier beyond.

He followed the oddly shod black again, across a sun-drenched lawn to the side of a large pool. A svelte dark girl in a blue swimsuit sat at a canopied crystal table by the pool.

The silent black turned and walked away. Adam hesi-tated, and went on toward the girl. She had leaned to stare at a gaudy butterfly hovering over her glass. Her lithe ivory body glistened with water, and her sleek hair was black and dripping. Rainbow colors flowed in it, where it had begun to dry.

"General Masters?"

Startled, the girl whirled to her feet. Equally startled, Adam recognized her long almond eyes and her vivid, heart-shaped face.

"Huh?" he gasped. "Dr. Ming!"

"Polly Ming, to you." She relaxed quickly, laughing at his confusion. "General Masters coming soon. Like Scotch-and-soda?"

Surprised but relieved to find her here, he joined her gladly at the crystal table. She looked younger and less severe than she had been on the moon. Her English seemed more fluent, though she still had a soft, exotic accent. No friend of contact, she was at least more appealing than the bull-necked sergeant. With a childlike delight, she was smiling at the gaudy yellow butterfly.

"Fantastic creatures here!"

"Polly Ming," he blurted urgently, "I want to ask some questions. Where are we? Who are those black men—and why are they all alike? What can you tell me about *Man First?*"

"Nothing, at moment." Her vivid face turned grave. "Though you know too much to leave us, exact status not yet settled."

Adam scowled at her. "Suppose I refuse to join?"

"Refusal not allowed." She bent toward him intimately. "Defiance not judicious now." Her husky voice turned provocative. "Like me, Adam? Perhaps we two make best of *Man First.*"

A barefoot black came silently from the bright-screened pavilion with two drinks on a tray. She trilled and clicked at him. He answered softly, set the glasses on the table, quietly withdrew.

"Drink, Adam! Drink to happy creature."

Gaily, she waved her glass toward the hovering butterfly.

"What is he?" Adam half rose, staring after the black. "I just looked at that red cap and his shoes. They—they're part of him. His foot's a sort of padded hoof!" A creeping terror shook his voice. "They're all alike—and they aren't men! Polly, what are they?"

She shrugged bewitchingly.

"Here's General. Will decide what you to know." Alluring in the tight suit, she flowed to her feet. "General Jett Masters. Adam Cave. New recruit, sir."

The general was a solidly muscular man, jauntily erect, tanned richly brown. His black shorts and silver T-shirt were authorized tropical gear for the Space Force but the patch on his chest was the black shield and white fist of *Man First.*

"Hullo, Cave."

Vigorously, he shook Adam's hand. Strong white teeth flashed through his quick dark smile. His face was angular and ugly, but Adam sensed ruthless force there.

"Knew your father." His voice was clipped, loud, coldly

metallic—and somehow familiar. "Because of him, we'll make a place for you."

Abruptly, Adam stood up again.

"You knew my father?" He caught a gasping breath. "I—I know your voice!" He stared at the stocky man. "You're Tom Jett!" he whispered accusingly. "You were with my father in the circumlunar station when it crashed on the moon."

"Actually, we were removed from the station before the crash." The general nodded briskly. "I escaped from the transgalactic contact team before they got us back to their chief. But I was there. I knew your father."

"Is he—is he still alive?"

"So far as I know." The general frowned, his narrowed eyes ice-blue in the caves beneath his black, jutting brows. "But we came to disagree on the advantages of contact. We have not been friends. I am not in touch with him."

"What hap—" Adam drew a sharp breath and tried to calm himself. "Out on the moon, I found the audio log of your contact with a ship from Tau Ceti," he whispered hoarsely. "What happened afterward?"

"Sit down, Cave."

The general gestured toward the pastel pavilion and waited for the sleek black man-thing that came running silently with another drink on a tray.

"You'll find out later, if you go along with us." His raspy voice crackled like the voice on the audio tape. "But right now we need to settle your position in *Man First.*"

"I'm not sure I want a place," Adam said. "I understand you oppose contact?"

"We're fighting contact." His dark, gaunt face set into a savage mask. "We're rooting out every rumor that contact may be possible." He grinned bleakly at the girl. "We sent Dr. Ming to the moon to kill Project Lifeline."

"But you were aboard the station." Bewildered, Adam shook his head. "You know that some kind of contact has already happened—"

"I've been through contact." Masters nodded. "That's precisely why I'm so bitter against the idea—why, in fact, that

I am using certain fruits of contact to limit further contact."

"What's so bad about it?" Adam leaned desperately across the crystal table. "My own family doesn't like it—I suppose because they're afraid of change. Is there a better reason?"

Something splashed behind him in the pool. Masters frowned in that direction, drumming absently on the table with bony, black-haired fingers.

"I'm not a bad man, Cave." The bleak pride had thawed from his face, and his abrupt earnest voice held an odd humility. "You may not like what I do, but I'm not entirely bad."

Adam waited, puzzled and uneasy.

"So far as I'm bad at all, I'm a living argument against transgalactic contact." His pale narrow eyes flashed disconcertingly at Adam. "Because I was once as innocent and eager as you appear to be. Your own father selected me, remember, to be his teammate on the project.

"Good or bad, contact made me what I am—"

Another splash interrupted him. Adam turned, watching for another swimmer, but nothing came out of the sloshing blue water. Polly Ming stood up quickly, looking at Masters.

"Am warm?" Her voice seemed oddly interrogative. "Taking dip?"

Masters nodded, and she dived as neatly as a young dolphin. Watching for her, Adam thought she was a long time coming up.

"I guess you'd like to know what the galaxies are like." Masters' harsh impatient voice demanded his attention. "People ask, but I can't tell. Suppose a monkey escaped from a space research lab. What could he tell his friends in the jungle about his travels?"

He scowled at the pool as if waiting for Polly to return.

"Do you mean—" Adam hesitated uneasily. "Do you mean contact was bad for you?"

"It changed me." Masters shrugged. "Your father doesn't like me now—nor do I like him. But you can't unhatch an egg. Let's just say I intend to protect the world from the same sort of change."

Adam didn't ask what sort of change.

"I used to be religious." Speaking only half to Adam, he seemed somehow compelled to explain and justify himself. "In a naïve way. I used to pray. But out in the galaxies I met creatures mightier and more magnificent than I had ever dreamed God could be. Creatures all but omnipotent, but no more moral than I am. Or should I say beyond morality?"

Moodily, he stared into the pool.

"I'd believed, of course, that I was psychologically prepared for contact. Your father and I used to talk about it. About definitions of mind and life. About the theoretical limits of intelligent power. About possible laws of universal ethics."

His thin lips twitched sardonically.

"But I guess I wasn't very well prepared—certainly not in the sense your father was. He accepted each new fact and being like a kid opening gifts at Christmas. But those terrible powers hit me differently. They mocked every goal and standard I used to value. I had to look for new laws of life." His pale eyes lifted, oddly eager, almost wistful.

"My new world is what I'm offering you. Because—" He leaned quickly across the table, somehow pathetic. "Because I need you, Cave. I'm a very lonely person. The other man who shared my experience has become my enemy. He would have destroyed me long ago—if his fantastic ethical notions had let him."

"My father—"

Grinning ironically, he lifted his hand to stop Adam's answer.

"Before you speak, let me sum things up. If you think my aims are bad—I see you do—they are bad only against the scale of a few microbes on one brief speck of cosmic dust. I failed to find your father's quixotic values justified anywhere else. I found no abstract galactic justice—nothing but the law of power."

His gaunt jaws tightened.

"That's my law. For me, that was the lesson of contact—that I had to increase myself, against everything that dwarfed me. Frankly, Cave, I intend to grasp and use whatever power I can find.

"Yet I say that I am not entirely bad, because I intend to protect the mass of men from all that contact did to me. In that sense, you may regard me as the greatest humanitarian. Greater even than your father."

He leaned toward Adam.

"I really need you, Cave. Without my experience, you can't imagine my predicament. Most human beings seem dull to me now. The genifacts are too limited, if not exactly stupid. Other creatures are too clever. I need to share my power with somebody like you—and I've power enough to share.

"What about it, Cave?"

"You know my answer," Adam said.

Masters' cold eyes flickered toward the pool. "If you're interested in Polly—"

"On her terms," Adam said. "Not on yours."

"They are the same." His dark face was cragged granite now. "You underestimate the power of transgalactic science. Power I want to share with you. All the power I once attributed to God! To create life. To control it, enrich it, extend it to immortality. Or to erase it—with no sense of sin."

An artery throbbed visibly in his gaunt throat.

"The genifacts are my own creation, to own or bestow. Take her, if you like." He grinned slowly, without mirth. "You can't fight me, Cave."

"I won't fight my father."

"Not without a better reason, eh?" Masters lowered his voice and widened his bleak grin, as trying to relax some ruthless force that drove him. "In fact, there is another reason to join *Man First* good enough at least for your uncles and Dr. Runescribe. I suppose I'll have to offer it to you."

He hesitated briefly, his angular head shrewdly tilted.

"I'm going to tell you the basic secret of *Man First*— a secret most of our own members don't know." That half-restrained fury began to gravel his voice again. "I have killed outsiders for suspecting it. The bare hint of it commits you to us for life."

"I'm not committed—"

"You are now!" A bright fanatic light glowed in Masters' sunken eyes. "The real danger we fight is nothing out of space. No invasion of bug-eyed monsters. No corruption of our human culture by contact with alien ideas. No extinction of the will to live through any desolating discovery that all our dreams were achieved on a million other worlds a billion years ago."

Ominously, Masters lifted his close-clipped skull.

"What we fight is a deadlier and more familiar danger, right here on Earth. *Man First* actually exists to put down the rebellion—the explosion—of the colored races here on Earth. We're preparing not for space war, but race war."

"So your real slogan is 'White Man First'?"

"Right." Masters nodded. "We are fighting for the survival of the white race. Knowing that, you can see the need of secrecy. Though our plans are moving fast, any breach of security could drench half the world with white blood. We already have influential members in every white group—including the Monk family." Bright teeth flashed through his sardonic grin. "Do you like us, Cave?"

"No!" Wondering how Polly Ming liked *Man First*, he glanced toward the pool. She had not emerged. "I want no part of any race war," he said. "Every race has equal rights, so far as I can see, and generally equivalent gifts. No race is superior."

"Objectively, of course you're right." Master tipped his ironic ugly head toward the pool. "I admire Polly Ming as much as you do. Objectively, in ways that count, she is certainly superior. But I'm not objective. I'm white."

"I believe in the brotherhood of men."

"A noble notion." Masters shrugged. "I was full of noble notions once. Racial toleration. Integration. Equal rights and brotherhood. The trouble is your little colored brothers never heard of all those noble notions."

Icy fire lit his eyes.

"They hate us, Cave. Just because we used to have white

71

power. Now they're getting power of their own. Black power. Yellow power. Brown power. Red power. They are breeding like vermin, swarming to crush us with blind, senseless colored power. I don't intend to be crushed.

"That, Cave, is the real reason for *Man First*."

Polly Ming had come out of the pool, seal-sleek, black hair plastered to her dripping head. As she passed the table, Masters slapped his arm around her tawny waist, possessively.

"A doubting Thomas, Polly. Tell him he's with us in *Man First* now."

"Is true, Adam." She nodded soberly. "Secret power existing to control non-white peoples. Membership sometimes involuntary."

"Polly is caught in between—that's her tragedy." Masters' black-haired arm tightened around her body. "She's Eurasian. Neither white nor dark. Cast out by both races, she belongs to me. Right, Polly?"

"Right, General." Her mobile mouth flashed an instant smile at Masters, but Adam caught the dark trouble in her eyes. Uncomfortably, full of a puzzled pity for her, he swung to the general.

"What has your notion of white superiority to do with transgalactic contact?"

"Everything." Masters gulped down his drink. "The parallel is perfect. The preachers of integrated human brotherhood are the same idiot mollycoddles who expect an eager welcome into some sort of transgalactic brotherhood. Equal rights for bug-eyed monsters!"

His dark lips twitched into a sneer.

"In *Man First*, we are realists," he said. "We recognize that competition for survival is the basic law of life. Here on Earth, we are not surprised when the preachers of black power burn a white man. Out in space, we expect no brotherly love from the aliens of any other planet."

"Have you really found hostility?" Adam demanded. "You and my father? That ship from Tau Ceti? Did it actually attack?"

"I believe you saw the wreckage on the moon." A cruel

fire lit Masters' eyes. "But we found something even more disturbing. That is the reluctance of any alien creature to recognize white superiority. To the worlds outside, black and white men look too much alike."

"I see," Adam muttered bitterly. "You're just like the Monks. Afraid of change. Afraid to risk the status quo."

"We are the status quo." That veiled violence surged again in Masters. "You can choose to join us—or else declare yourself a stinking traitor to your own white race. In either case, I've wasted time enough—"

Masters checked his strident voice. Grinning thinly, he lifted one lean finger. The golden-branded man-thing came running with three fresh drinks on a tray. Adam studied the creature, from red-black coxcomb to black-padded hoof.

"What are they?" A wave of horror choked his voice. "They look—inhuman."

"They aren't human." Masters had recovered his control. "They're our genifacts. Genetic artifacts. Manufactured to fit our peculiar needs. Without them, *Man First* might seem a forlorn cause. With them, we are unbeatable."

"You—you created them?" Adam shivered. "You can create men?"

"They're not quite men, though we used human genes to make them. For our uses, they're better than men. Better, because of their limits. Absolutely loyal, because they are absolutely simple. None of the complexities that can make a doubting Thomas or a traitor of the best of men."

His sardonic eyes flickered at Adam.

"You'll need to know their special gifts. One is a sense for treason. They can smell it out before the potential traitor is aware of it himself. They weed out the weak sisters. I think they will help keep you loyal."

"No!" Adam's voice came with a hoarse force that he had not intended. "I'll never join you."

"Your reluctance is not surprising." Masters seemed alertly calm. "I'm prepared to make concessions, because you are important to us. Let me explain your special function in *Man First*."

He waited warily.

"Speaking of your father—I see a likeness now." Masters grinned across his lifted drink. "He's still trying to fight *Man First*. Living in hiding. Gathering a few tattered disciples. Preaching his insane brotherhood of men and monsters. Our efforts to silence him have evidently failed. You're to play Judas to him."

Adam recoiled from him, speechless.

"Write your own check. Power, Polly, money, whatever. You'll find discipline in *Man First*, but also generosity. A hard stick. But tasty carrots, too. Are you with us, Cave?"

Trembling, Adam shook his head.

"Stubborn as your father!" A quick impish smile gave an unexpected charm to Masters' fleshless face. "I like your loyalty, but it's misdirected." He leaned persuasively across the table. "James Cave has become a wild fanatic. Dangerous to more than *Man First*. He wants to break all the barriers. Mix men and monsters. He has got to be stopped."

Sweatily, Adam clutched the cold rim of the crystal table. He stared at Masters, alarmed by that flash of crooked charm. He glanced at Polly's long exotic eyes, still perplexed about her place in *Man First*. He groped desperately for some sane plan of action.

All he found was hopeless bewilderment.

"I know it's hard." Masters smiled again, appealingly. "You can't refuse, but I hope you join us willingly. I'll give you time to reconsider. Perhaps Polly can persuade you. But we've other business now."

"Wait!" Adam felt trapped in a web he couldn't understand. "I didn't ask for this—"

"But you did." Masters was on his feet, bluntly crisp again. "You volunteered for Project Lifeline, against the advice of your family. You dug up that audio log. You got yourself involved with enemy agents on the moon and brought a spy device to Earth. You tried to break arrest. Men have been eliminated for less. Think about it, Adam." He turned impatiently. "Or perhaps you'd rather feed the tripus!"

He stalked off toward the pool, without explaining. Adam

looked at Polly Ming, hoping in spite of all he had seen for some hint of friendship or aid, but she had risen with Masters, dark eyes downcast. She followed to the pool. Masters glanced into the water and beckoned brusquely at the waiting genifact.

Staring after them, Adam trembled with a savage need for action. He felt like a mouse in a circle of cats. He had been tempted and toyed with too long, pushed around beyond endurance. His groping efforts to learn where he stood had only led him deeper into wild nightmare. He wanted to fight, even if he failed. His fists clenched and quivered.

But how was he to fight? Despair poured like a cold flood over him. He had no friend—if Polly Ming couldn't aid him. He had no weapon or plan. Utterly lost, he didn't even know what continent this was.

Fleetingly, he thought of saying he would join. Polly's ivory grace made alluring bait—but he shied from the trap. Even if surrender led him to survival, a doubtful case, that was the way Masters had gone. He refused to become another Masters—

Something splashed in the pool.

Masters peered into the heaving water and gestured sharply for the genifact to dive. The naked black man-thing stood poised at the brink, piping softly. Polly whispered a quick protest. Masters yelled an order. The creature dived.

"Think it over." Masters swung briefly back to him. "Think fast."

He strolled away toward the bright pastel pavilion, his muscular arm around Polly. His lowered voice murmured to her. They didn't look back.

The splashing in the pool was suddenly furious. Spray glittered in the sun. The flying drops turned red. Unwillingly, as if an icy coil of nightmare had reached out to seize him, Adam stumbled across the sun-baked tile to the pool.

Scarlet froth covered the uneasy water. At first he saw nothing else. Then something yellow-and-black-and-crimson drifted up through the boiling red murk. The genifact's torso, headless, still bound with a torn scrap of the yellow loincloth.

He recoiled from it, stifled a cry.

The water heaved. Something leaped. A flying image that burned into his brain. Something black and corrugated, washed with dripping red. Something shark-sized, but shaped like an impossible octopus with three sleekly tapered tentacles.

It arched high, shimmering in the sun, as lithely graceful as Polly Ming. He felt it looking at him with three small bright hooded eyes spaced about its corrugated crown. He had time to flinch from its probing stare, his flesh crawling.

Its crown opened, three corrugated triangles rolling back like the petals of a hideous flower. The bulbed body was bright pink inside, the triple jaw set with hooked black fangs. A barbed scarlet tongue stabbed out, round and powerful as a striking python, drooling slime.

That tongue speared the morsel. The triple jaw snapped on it. Crown first, muscular tentacles trailing, the whole creature vanished in pink spray. It left a sweetish fetor like the presence of death.

It was the tripus. His shaken brain recognized that. Masters had deliberately let him see it feeding. Shuffling backward from its evil odor, he thought of Polly's dip with it. He stood swaying, utterly unnerved.

Something touched his arm. He gasped and jumped and whirled. Another genifact had come up behind him, the tall black twin of the diver. It chittered gently, tugging at his sleeve. He caught his breath and followed it toward the elevator.

Beyond the bright-roofed building and the dark wall of trees, a climbing jet leaped like a tiny silver fish into the milky tropic sky. A sonic boom battered him. He fell to his knees and came up clutching a white-painted stone from the curb of the path.

He dared not look back, but Masters and Polly must have had time to reach the building. The proudly marching genifact was now a dozen yards ahead. Neatly mowed turf stretched out to the vine-hung forest wall. The naked creature paused ahead, as if to turn.

He caught his breath and threw the rock.

Desperately, he darted for the woods. A strange low cry followed him. From the corner of the building, he glanced behind him. The black stood holding the rock, which it must have caught in its hand. Its narrow face seemed to show a mild amazement. It was trilling at him gently.

He ducked and ran frantically. Its muffled footfalls came behind him. It didn't throw the rock, but some smaller object like a purple grape flashed past his head and exploded with a pale blue flash when it struck the grass.

He caught an odor like plastic glue—

He woke on the cot in that gray cell. A thin, sickly reek of plastic glue clung around him. A dull ache throbbed in his head. He found a tender bruise on his temple, where perhaps he had fallen against a curb.

He sat up gingerly, stifling a groan. The soundproof door was sealed again. He had accomplished nothing, he thought bitterly, except to show his helpless panic.

For a time he paced the cell, trying to imagine ways to break out, to reach his father in hiding, to help defeat *Man First*, to restore some useful contact with the interstellar culture. But his imagination failed. He was dozing on the cot again, when he heard the door and saw Polly Ming.

"Unhappy, Adam?" she murmured huskily. "Unhappy, too?"

"Why should I be happy?" He lurched from the cot toward the steel door, but it had already thudded softly shut behind her. "I've bungled everything."

"Unhappy to see me?"

"Not if you can get me out of here."

She came flowing from the door on little sandaled feet. A black lace kimono heightened her lithe allure. Gold and yellow fire played across her sleek black hair. He tried not to think of her swim with the tripus.

"Cannot aid escape." She swayed so close that her heady

77

perfume enveloped him. "General Masters commands persuasion. Must join us in *Man First!*"

Heart thudding, he looked her up and down. With an ironic smile of approval, he pulled her hard against him and kissed her yielding mouth. He pushed her roughly away and sat down on the cot, laughing harshly.

"Why the laughing?" Her long eyes looked hurt. "Dislike me?"

"I like you fine," he said. "But you remind me of a girl I can't marry now—a girl I'll probably never see again. You remind me of all I really want—to get out of here, and find my father, and beat *Man First*—"

Swiftly, frightened, she laid a finger on her mouth.

She paused to peer around the gray concrete room in a way that made him think of General Monk searching for hidden bugs.

"Black genifacts are smallest power of *Man First*," she informed him swiftly. "Are also such antisocial creatures as tripus."

There was no time to ask why she swam with the tripus, but he rejoiced to see that she did not approve it.

"Are stranger powers. Drugs of the mind. Mental states in plastic tubes, ready for injection. Instant truth or instant madness. Holy Inquisition in a needle. Courage to feed tripus in little pill. Loyalty to *Man First* disguised in cup of coffee. General says he sought God once, found omnipotence in bottles."

An elfin smile lit her tawny face.

"Drug to make you love me, Adam. More than you love contact." She glided toward him, her voice dropping cautiously. "General now meeting advisers. Your case on agenda. Are three alternatives for you. Perhaps I persuade you to join *Man First*. Conscious choice. Perhaps drugs persuade you. Chemical choice. Perhaps you feed tripus. No choice.

"Is time for choice—"

Laughing hoarsely, he reached up to seize her hands. "No problem, Polly." He pulled her down into his arms. "I choose you."

When he kissed her, a hard, round object came through

her parted lips into his mouth. He drew sharply back. She clung warmly to him.

"Not speak!" He heard an urgent warning in her whisper. "Not talk now!"

He didn't speak.

When she was gone through the heavy door, with a wary finger at her lips, he went into the shower stall before he slipped the object from his mouth. It was a heavy platinum hongkong coin from the People's Moon Republic —precisely like the device that Jason Caine had given him.

Fingers abruptly shuddering and numb, he gripped the two faces. He twisted them, one against the other. Harder. Harder. Something clicked. One face turned on the other, clicked again.

"Forgive me!" he breathed. "Forgive me, Polly Ming."

VI

HE TURNED THE shower on. Under cover of its splash and hiss, he held the almond-eyed Freedom on the coin an inch from his lips and whispered breathlessly:

"Adam Cave to Jason Caine. Answer softly, if you hear me—my cell is bugged! Adam Cave to Jason—"

"Cave, huh?" The Freedom spoke, in a twangy, far-off voice. "What's skinning you?"

Gasping to a colder shock than the water gave him, he recognized the diminished nasal voice.

"Smith!" He almost forgot to whisper. "Solomon Smith?"

"Once attached to Project Lifeline," the Freedom creaked. "Now with Jason Caine. Sorry about the hairy trick I played you on the moon. Couldn't help it then. Where the skin are you?"

"At a *Man First* jetport in a forest that looks tropical,"

Adam breathed. "I don't know where. Local time probably late afternoon—but I've been nerve-bombed, so even that is just a guess. I'm locked in an underground cell—"

"Keep your skin on," Smith interrupted him. "Don't risk more talk. Leave the transceiver open as you have it. Hide it in your mouth. We'll get a fix and home in on it. Better continue normal routine—just for the bugs."

He put the hongkong back in his mouth. Though he had no normal routine, he deliberately finished the shower, toweled himself, stood at the mirror to inspect the purpling bruise on his temple. He wandered out to the bar and punched for ice water.

Lifting the paper cup, he caught a lingering sickish scent of plastic glue. Sudden terror dashed the water from his lips. Was it already laced with instant loyalty to *Man First?*

He had no wish to test it.

His fearful start had spilled the water, but he reflected that his watchers could not expect a man in his place to be notably calm. Trying not to tremble, he mopped the floor with a tissue, disposed tissue and cup, walked unsteadily back to the cot.

"Spaceman Cave!" The hard male voice rapped from the bare gray wall. "General Masters is ready for your case. He wants to know if you have been persuaded to support *Man First.*"

"Noth yeth—" Taken by surprise, he coughed and bent his head while he moved the hongkong to his cheek. "Not yet," he muttered rustily. "This whole situation is so unexpected. I need more time to think about it."

"I'll report your reply," the wall said. "But the general won't put up with delay."

Unable to imagine what sort of help might come when Smith homed in the hongkong, or when it might arrive, he wanted to wait at the door. Instead, he lay down circumspectly on the cot and fixed his eyes on the low gray ceiling. Listening for some sound of hope, he heard only the fast march of his own anxious pulse.

To ease the ruthless tension, to shield himself from the shapes of danger he didn't know and the hopes he couldn't quite visualize, he let half his mind go back to Polly Ming. He tried to balance her exotic Eurasian enchantment against the clean athletic charm of Kayren Hunter. Suppose he had to choose between them?

But of course he had already chosen. Kayren was known reality and common sense, the comfortable tradition of the familiar past, the best bit of his own world. He had already left her behind, along with Joseph Runescribe and the Monks. Polly was her opposite, pure romance, as darkly mysterious and unpredictable as his own future—if he had a future. He felt a painful ache of loss for Kayren, an excited anticipation for Polly. He wondered what dangers from Masters and *Man First* she had risked to bring him the hongkong, and wondered whether he would ever know—

"Spaceman Cave!"

His taut body jerked back from the hard crack of the voice from the wall.

"General Masters has closed your case. Prepare to leave your quarters. The genifacts are coming for you."

Fists clenching instinctively, he swung to his feet. The brittle voice was hint enough of what the genifacts would do with him. He slammed his hopeless weight against the unyielding door, then stumbled aimlessly into the tiny bath—

A soft animal whine spun him around.

He saw the massive door swinging slowly open. Three sleek black genifacts stood in the corridor beyond. These were armed. Two wore queer weapons strapped to their naked thighs. The leader had drawn something that had a dull blue gleam like the barrel of a gun. It was aimed—but not at him.

"Skin!" The voice of Solomon Smith was a breathless yelp. "Scramble in!"

For one wasted fraction of a second, he thought Smith's voice had come from the hongkong in his mouth. Dazed, he spat the coin toward his palm. Then he saw Smith himself.

Something like a stubby, square-hulled boat was floating beside him in the cell, a foot off the floor. It had a cock-

81

pit where Smith stood half-erect, pushing back a transparent bubble and leaning out to snatch at him.

With a movement half reflex, he flung the hongkong. It struck the arrogant inhuman face of the first genifact, fell jangling to the floor. Crouching back into the doorway, the creature fired.

He had dived for the cockpit. Violet lightning flickered around him. A dull thud jarred him. Something smashed him hard against the cockpit. The genifacts came after him, chittering softly.

"Skin 'em!"

Smith hauled him over the coaming and slammed the bubble shut. The genifacts were all shooting now, but Smith was crouching, clawing at a green-glowing panel. The musical chatter of the genifacts and the thudding of the queer guns faded into a breathless stillness. The gray cell turned dim and slid away.

"Hairy scrape!" Smith muttered. "You okay?"

He caught his breath, touched the stinging wetness on his jaw, rubbed his numb shoulder.

"Just cut and bruised, I guess."

Stunned from more than just that impact, he sat up beside Smith and tried to collect himself. The dim green shine of unfamiliar instruments lit the inside of the bubble. Outside, a fainter glow outlined the stubby hull. Beyond, all he saw was a wall of suffocating blackness.

"No, you ain't crazy." Smith turned from the instruments, with a one-sided grin. "But you do look like you need a drink."

He fumbled under the padded seat and came up with a flat brown bottle.

"Tequila," he said. "Gift of our new friends at Quinto del Rey. Hot as skin, but a man can learn to drink it." He uncapped the bottle and passed it to Adam. "Not like my own making," he added regretfully. "But Caine gave me no time to salvage my still at the project."

Adam took one fiery sip and blew to cool his throat.

"So you're with Jason Caine?" he whispered huskily.

"He picked me up on the moon." Smith rubbed the top

of the bottle with his palm and gulped noisily. "When I left you in the crater-crawler. A hairy trick—but we couldn't take a chance on you then."

Adam refused another drink.

"My father?" He peered urgently at Smith. "Do you know my father? Is he really still alive?"

"I know him." Smith paused, frown-lines biting into his angular face. "You'll find him alive—very anxious to see his son."

"Why the frown?" Alarm caught Adam's voice. "Is—is something wrong?"

"He's ill." Smith gulped again, capped the brown bottle, stowed it under the seat. "Some virus he picked up in space. Harmless to the higher races, but dangerous to us." His glass-green eyes stabbed sharply at Adam. "Seems our friends in *Man First* are partly right," he added wryly. "Transgalactic contact ain't all good."

"Where is my father now?"

"Here on Earth," Smith said. "Wanted to come home. You'll see him today."

"There's so much to ask about." Adam stared at Smith, and out into the smothering dark. "Tell me—tell me about this vehicle!"

"Caine taught me how to punch the buttons, but don't ask me how it works." Smith bent to inspect a dial, adjusted something on the green-lit panel, leaned back in the seat. "It's a landing craft. From the starship. It pretty well operates itself."

"Even underground?"

"An incidental effect of what Caine calls the FTL drive." Smith's bottle-green eyes squinted at him shrewdly. "The starships go faster than light. That means they have to get around what Caine calls the Relativity Barrier."

"They actually do that?" The staggering fact took Adam's breath. "General Kalinin will be surprised to know the limit can be broken."

"He'll be surprised." Smith grinned maliciously. "Though the limit ain't exactly broken. Caine tried to tell me how they get around it. You understand the theoretical barrier?"

"Mass increases with speed." Adam nodded. "At the speed of light, mass would be infinite. All the power in the universe couldn't push a ship that fast—not according to Einstein and Kalinin."

"Skin me if I can follow the math, but they do get around it," Smith said. "Through some sort of mathematical hyperspace outside our universe. The device field rotates the mass of each individual atom partly or entirely out of our space. Mass and momentum are adjustable, all the way to zero. One of Kalinin's ants could carry a rotated ship."

He twisted to point at an armored bulge behind the seat.

"The actual drive is a set of rotors spinning in a differential field, with a vector thrust from mass increasing on one side and decreasing on the other. Caine insists there's no violation of Newton's third law—but ask him if you want to know what they push against!"

"That's out in space." Adam shook himself, blinking into the walling dark. "But we're underground?"

"Rotated atoms slide through other matter," Smith said. "Pretty essential for a starship, that otherwise couldn't help hitting cosmic junk at several times the speed of light. I was able to home in your signal, straight through the crust of the Earth."

Adam sat silent for half a minute, trying to grasp the fact that they were really deep inside the Earth. He felt staggered with all the implications of contact, too deeply wonderstruck even to ask the right questions.

"What is it like?" he demanded at last. "Out on those other worlds?"

"Ask your father," Smith said. "He has been there."

A red light had begun to wink on the panel. He bent to move a lever. A moment later, Adam saw the darkness beyond the bubble become a ghostly gray. It brightened to a midnight blue, broke suddenly into a blaze of sun on running waves.

Squinting against the blinding dazzle, he saw a dingy open boat pitching on the waves below their hovering craft. Two dark men, naked to the waist, were trailing hand lines into the glittering water. Smith lifted the bubble to hail the fishermen.

"Pedro! Chino! Here's our new disciple. He has proved himself skinnish well. Now he's come to see his father."

The taller man stood up skillfully to help him step into the boat. He wore steel-rimmed glasses on a dark, proud, hook-nosed face.

"We are honored, *señor*." His smiled showed dark, broken teeth. "If your father is *El Contactor!*"

Adam sat carefully on a splintered thwart and looked back at Smith. The stubby landing craft had become a ghostly outline. In an instant there was only the sunlit sea and a far brown haze of land and a dazzle of cumulus clouds building in the milky sky.

Chino was a laughing, stocky man with Chinese features and the color of a Negro. He toiled to start the rusty inboard engine, while Pedro coiled the thick hand lines.

"Dom' sonabeech!" Chino grinned cheerfully. "The engine, eet 'as no contact!"

"You are wounded, *señor?*"

Pedro was leaning anxiously to examine the cut on Adam's jaw, which was stiffening now with drying blood.

"A scratch." He shrugged. "Nothing serious. Tell me about my father."

"Your father's wound may have been no more than that." Pedro washed the cut with stinging seawater and stuck an adhesive bandage over it.

"Where is he now?" Adam asked.

"*Allá.*" He gestured toward the hazed horizon. "His coming honors our small *caserío*. We have been very poor. Our village, like the world, had a sickness of the soul. *El Contactor* brings hope to Quinta del Rey."

The balky engine coughed and began throbbing steadily. Chino turned the boat toward the bright pile of cloud and the brown streak of land. Pedro sat reflectively rubbing the salt spray from his glasses.

"*Un dia de verdad.*" He smiled solemnly at Adam. "A great day of truth. Our world has need of truth, because as people say our gods are dead. *Mi bisabuelo*—how do you say—my great-grandfather was a Jewish rabbi. My grandfather was an atheist whose god was Marx. My own father was baptized a Christian, but put his real faith in *el progreso.*"

His naked, sunburned shoulders shrugged them all away.

"I had no belief," he said. "God and Marx are dead. Progress is only for the rich. Look at Quinta del Rey."

He waved his glasses toward the blur of land.

"The new dams up on the *sierra* take all the water from our river. The new office of *turismo* sends all the rich *gringos* to greater places. The new electronic trawlers take all the fish out of the sea. That is progress!"

He glanced sadly down into the empty boat.

"*Nada por los pobres.* For the poor there is nothing. I had no religion, because I had found no love or justice in the world—until your father came. Now he is my religion."

The hamlet of Quinta del Rey rose slowly from the sea. A straggle of dusty palms. A cluster of low adobe huts. The broken stone walls of an old mission on the stony hill behind it.

Chino steered the boat through a white roar of surf, and both barefoot men jumped out to beach it on a scrap of white sand. Pedro guided Adam to a blue-painted door in the village.

"*Su padre.*" His black teeth smiled. "*Es aquí.*"

In the cool gloom of the narrow, earth-floor room, a man lay on a bed of palm-fronds covered with a faded blanket. A neat dark girl in trim black-and-silver stood over the bed, fanning the flies away with a dry palm leaf.

"Hiya, Adam!" Fine teeth flashed through her friendly smile. Startled, he saw that she was the black Swan he had met on the moon. "Your father is sleeping."

"Awake now." The man sat up on the bed. "Want to see my son."

Leaning back against the whitewashed wall, he held up his hand for Adam to shake. His deep-toned drawl was somehow familiar. In a moment, Adam recognized the bright blue eyes and the flowing yellow hair.

"Caine!" He stood frozen for a moment, before he could take the lifted hand. "Jason Caine! *You're* my father?"

He clung to the quivering hand, dazed and wounded by the change in the vigorous athlete he had met in the centrifuge at the Tycho Hilton. The eyes were deeply sunk, the fair skin pinched and pale."

"I had to use a different name." Even the deep voice seemed weakened and uneven. "Because *Man First* is hunting us. But I am your father."

"You knew me?" Adam whispered. "You knew me on the moon?"

"I had kept up with you," Caine nodded. "But I couldn't trust you then. You were still too close to the Monks. *Man First* has given us too many heartbreaking surprises. But Smith says we can trust you now."

"You can," Adam said.

"A staggering trust!" Caine's haggard eyes weighed him. "If you're big enough, you can help settle the whole future of our world—in the transgalactic culture or outside of it." The sick man paused, frowning at him doubtfully. "Can you tackle that?"

"I'll try," Adam said. "I do believe in the benefits of contact—"

"Hold on!" Caine raised his shaking, wasted hand. "You know nothing about contact. When you do know something, the decision won't be so easy. But anyhow I like your attitude. I'm proud you're my son."

Caine hitched himself back on the pile of dusty palm leaves, to sit higher against the adobe wall. He rested for a moment, his dark-rimmed eyes fondly weighing Adam.

"Tell me," Adam urged him. "Tell me what I need to know."

"I'll tell you what I can," Caine said. "But then you'll have to make your own decisions."

He paused again, hesitantly biting a fever-cracked lip. Adam saw a bright fleck of blood. The black Swan stooped anxiously to adjust a pillow behind his head. She tried to wipe his lip with a cloth.

"No matter." He waved her off impatiently. "Find a seat for my son."

Silently, she left the room. Caine lay back against the pillow with his sunken eyes closed. Adam thought he had gone to sleep, but he aroused himself with a visible effort when the girl came back with a little wicker stool for Adam.

"Contact has been my goal since I was a boy—long before Tom Jett and I were picked up off the moon." His voice was husky and weak, yet carefully deliberate. "I have been studying the cosmic culture and learning the conditions of contact and trying to arrange to bring Earth into the transgalactic society. It isn't as simple as you might expect. In fact, you'll have to consider the possibility that Jett is right."

"I don't like him," Adam muttered. "Or his *Man First* mob."

"Some people do." Caine paused to draw a heavy breath. "And you'll find other enemies of contact, as dangerous as Jett and the Monks. There are theoretical opponents of progress outside, as well as on the Earth, who feel that our fine primitive culture should be protected from corruption by contact. There are even creatures that would exterminate us to make space for themselves.

"But my own illness is what shakes my faith."

Caine rubbed his cracked lip and sat staring grimly at the bright stain of blood on his fingers.

"Our cosmic friends have mastered the sciences of life," he whispered, so faintly that Adam bent forward to listen. "They can mold life like clay. They can create and manipulate genes, to design new kinds of life. They have wiped out illness and old age and unwanted death—among their own races. They promised me something close to immortality."

Sadly, wearily, almost bitterly, he shook his heavy head.

"I fell ill just a few days ago—in fact, while you were still on the moon. Our transgalactic friends seemed to be as much surprised and disturbed as I was. With all their science, they can't cure me. They can't even explain why they can't."

Adam stood up impulsively.

"Can't we do better than this?" He shrugged impatiently at the palm-leaf bed on the swept earth floor and the patient Swan fanning at the flies. "Let's get you to a good hospital."

"I tried that first," Caine said. "The day I fell sick I went to the new clinic of space medicine at Tycho City. The specialists there decided I had a hopeless type of radiation-leukemia. They said I'd be dead in a week."

His bleeding lips set bitterly.

"Even that wasn't good enough for them," he whispered hoarsely. "The clinic director turned out to be a member of *Man First*. Somehow he learned or guessed who I am. My sickness wasn't working fast enough to suit him. He tried to poison me.

"Fortunately, our friends have infiltrated *Man First*. They discovered the plot. Smith snatched me out of the clinic and brought us to Quinta del Rey." He paused to smile affectionately at the quiet black Swan. "Here at least I'm among the people I trust."

"Can't anything be done?" Adam turned restively to the girl with the fan, and back to Caine. "What do the space people have to say about your case?"

"A benign virus, they say—benign to them!" Caine grinned faintly. "Something they think I picked up on some outside planet. It ought to be harmless, but they think it has mutated in my body. They're treating me, but they say I don't respond."

He sat staring up at Adam, his eyes glazed and haunted and fever-bright.

"I'm not responding," he muttered hoarsely. "Contact is killing me. Suppose it kills the race? I don't mean just with this mutant virus—our friends insist that it has adapted itself to my body, so that it won't spread. But suppose there's something else, just as unexpected? Suppose it turns out that men can't bear to know the truth about their very humble place in the transgalactic universe? Suppose they don't respond?"

Painfully, he hitched his sagging body up again.

"That's the sort of nut you'll have to crack," he muttered. "You won't find it easy. Because contact is now a fact. We can't just erase the blackboard, or turn the clock back." His sick eyes examined Adam again. "Still want to take my place?"

Adam leaned forward eagerly.

"Trust me, Father." He paused to repeat the word, as if he had never spoken it before. "Father. Father!" He reached impulsively to grasp his father's hot and wasted hand. "Brief me," he urged. "Tell me what I need to know."

"You heard our audio log," Caine said. "You know how the contact began. Our signals from the project had reached the worlds of Tau Ceti. The starship came from a contact station there. Its crew picked us up beyond the moon, and arranged the crash to keep their secret until the conditions of contact could be met."

"What are they like?" Adam demanded. "Those creatures outside?"

"How can I tell you?" Caine hesitated, his hollowed eyes fixed on things far beyond the whitewashed walls.

"The transgalactic culture—" Silent again, he shook his wasted head. "It's old, Adam. If you date the cosmic culture from the introduction of the FTL drive—which makes it possible for life and ideas to spread from star to star—that introduction happened in our local cluster of galaxies about five billion years ago. Though the facts get a little vague across that span of time, the beginnings seem to have come from another cluster, older still."

"The beings?" Adam whispered. "The people—are they like us?"

"Some of them resemble us—in some ways. On an infinite number of worlds, you get every possible form of life. Most forms are strange. From our provincial point of view, some of them are shocking."

The black Swan had brought him a blue pottery bowl of a steaming liquid. It looked like tea, but it filled the room with a peppery pungence that stung Adam's eyes. Caine sipped it without enthusiasm.

"During my own education, I must have toured twenty

stellar systems," he said. "I have no time or strength to try to catalog the creatures I met, but perhaps I can tell you something about the crew of the starship that picked us up."

"Please!" Adam urged him eagerly. "It's hard to grasp so much at once."

"The chief officer—the one I'll call the inspector—was selected for human-like traits and a high quotient of appeal to human beings. No creatures in our own galaxy came close enough. The inspector—the whole contact team, in fact—comes from the star swarm we call the Greater Magellanic Cloud. The inspector can pass for a human being, but the others might have strayed out of a nightmare."

The black Swan had returned with a bottle of Carta Blanca for Adam. He accepted it mechanically. Vaguely, he knew that the warm beer was foaming down over his fingers, but he forgot to drink it. He was looking at the fearful, graceful image of the tripus burnt into his brain.

"The creature you might call the captain of the starship looks slightly like a six-foot pineapple. Though he can move himself and manipulate objects, his evolutionary origins must have been what we would call vegetable. He—or is it she?"

Caine paused, with a pale grin.

"Our old notions of sex begin to seem naïve. Evolution uses some such function nearly everywhere to produce varied crops of offspring from which the fittest survive. But that goal is reached by a range of means you can't imagine."

He smiled at the black Swan, accepting another sip from her pungent bowl.

"The captain disturbed me at first. But we got to be good friends. He—or she—has a compassionate understanding of the problems of an infant culture in first contact. A sense of humor, too—though I had a hard time learning to get the jokes."

He chuckled feebly at some unspoken recollection.

"The being you'd call the first mate looks like a cloud of bright blue smoke in motion and like a black solid at rest. He—or perhaps I'll have to say *it*—is made of unspecialized mobile cells, living in a free association. It thinks like a computer and knows nearly everything about the transgalactic culture.

"The second mate is also the navigator of the starship. It looks and sounds a little like a swarm of bees—except that the bees are silver-colored metal, and not bees at all. It's a communication specialist.

"The third mate's the thing that gives me the shakes. If you can imagine the ultimate killer. Half-bright metal. Half-alive. Shaped like a flying snake. Deadly enough to run down a war rocket or dive on a nuclear sub or dig up a bomb shelter. Quick and crafty enough to outwit anything. Bristling with hideous weapons, yet sleek and compact and somehow beautiful—"

Caine had stopped, his glazed eyes staring as if he saw the thing. His swollen, blood-beaded lips compressed, slowly relaxed again. His fever-bright eyes returned ironically to Adam, who sat trying not to think of the tripus.

"If you can imagine that—and then imagine the thing as friendly and playful as an intellectual dolphin. Making me translate Shakespeare and John Donne. Getting excited about the sonnet as a literary form. Finally even composing a cycle of metaphysical sonnets in its own peculiar archaic English—that gives you an idea of the third mate.

"Just a hint of the variation you'll find in transgalactic life. You have to remember that those creatures are special friends of ours, all devoted to their culture to new peoples. An unselfish missionary effort. The galaxy is full of stranger and less friendly things."

Such as the tripus, Adam thought. He let the black Swan take away his untasted beer. Staring at the sick man, he was trying hard to put the stunning facts of contact into some sane order.

"What about government?" he asked suddenly. "Who rules the galaxies?"

"Nobody," Caine said. "There is too much respect for difference—racial or individual. I suppose every possible social arrangement has been tried, but the society we have to deal with, here in our own contact, is a sheltered anarchy."

"Anarchy?"

"The citizens of the cosmos are a little like Thoreau," he said. "They dislike belonging to anything they didn't join. They regard coercive government in about the same way as you regard ceremonial mutilation—as a crude and cruel social artifact of the primitive past."

"But don't they have an organization?"

"There is something—for want of a better word, I'll call it the 'Club.' It offers everything from first aid to education to people who need its help, but it doesn't meddle with people who choose to live apart. Contributions to it are voluntary, and actual membership is privilege hard to win."

Adam sat frowning doubtfully.

"Anarchy seems somehow—impractical."

"A transgalactic republic or a transgalactic empire would be even more impractical," Caine answered. "A coercive nation trying to administer one percent of the inhabited galaxies would fall of its own dead weight."

Feeling lost in that transgalactic vastness, Adam turned to look for relief in the human reality of the black Swan. He thought wistfully of their meeting on the moon, and the steak they had never cooked.

One ancestor, she had told him proudly, had been a Matabele chief who died defending his kraal. Her own father had died in the tunnels of Tycho City, at the fall of the People's Moon Republic. Afterward her mother had worn out the rest of her life in the ice-mines, because freedom was only for the powerful.

Now she answered his glance with a grave little smile, but he saw the glow of complete devotion that lit her fine sloe eyes when she looked back at his father. Jason Caine, he saw, was her religion.

"Something closer home." Heartened by that glimpse of the Swan's faith, he turned quickly back to his father. "What are these conditions of contact that we must meet?"

"The Club has been watching us." Caine's worn voice was deliberately precise. "Ever since they located Earth as the cradle of a viable new culture. That happened, I think,

93

some millions of years ago. The conditions are laid down by the Club, for our protection. They follow from a guiding principle of self-determination."

He waited while the Swan adjusted the pillow at his back.

"The first condition is simply that contact must be initiated by men on Earth, not by any beings outside." His voice grew fainter. "We've already satisfied that condition, of course, with our signals from Project Lifeline."

Relaxing against the pillow, Caine closed his haggard eyes. The Swan touched her lips and shook her head when Adam tried to prompt him, but in a moment his slow, careful voice toiled on.

"The second condition is that contact must be requested by a team from Earth which has studied the transgalactic culture. Tom Jett and I composed that team. Unfortunately, we disagreed."

"And he came back to start *Man First*," Adam put in. "He's General Jett Masters now."

"Try converting Tom!" Caine gave him a yellow, twisted grin. "There is a third condition," he added huskily. "Full contact cannot be opened without the approval of the Club inspector in charge."

"Will he approve?"

"Approval has been delayed these many years," Caine said. "Because of my disagreement with Jett. But I have asked the inspector to visit us tonight, here at Quinta del Rey. Jett's recent conduct has given us some new arguments, but my illness casts a shadow over our case. I hope for a decision tonight, one way or the other."

Uncertainly, he shook his hollowed head.

"I can't guess which way."

"After that?" Adam asked. "What next?"

"Depends on the inspector," Caine muttered. "Finally, perhaps, on you. If the inspector disapproves contact, I suppose the Club ship will return to its Tau Ceti base. Anyhow we'll be left in isolation—I can't guess how long."

"But if contact is approved?"

"Then it's up to us." His haunted eyes dwelt on Adam.

"To my few disciples, if I am dead by then." He moved a thin hand, to silence Adam's protest. "The conditions don't allow our friends to interfere. All they can do is give us advice and artifacts. We'll have to plant the new culture ourselves. In defiance of Tom Jett and *Man First*—"

His voice changed to a gasping snore. He slipped off the pillow and toppled sidewise. The Swan stooped quickly to catch his head. She straightened his gaunt head and wiped his blood-flecked lips and put Adam out of the room.

Lost again, he wandered out into the suffocating afternoon, groping blindly for some sort of mental bridge from this poor *caserío* to the transgalactic culture. The high sun made dazzling brass of sea and beach and sky. Two dark archways frowned down from the shattered walls of the abandoned mission on the hill, like empty sockets in an old god's skull. The ragged palms drooped, without life or motion, bleached colorless in the glare. Fat blue flies buzzed around the swollen corpse of a gray rat stinking in a muddy rut. A naked brown boy of five or six came solemnly down the street, walking quickly in the molten sunlight and slowly in the narrow strips of shade. When Adam smiled, he nodded gravely and went on. Adam stopped at the end of the dusty street, feeling discouraged and confused. The gulf ahead seemed too wide and deep for anything to bridge.

The fisherman, Pedro, overtook him there. Freshly scrubbed and shaven, attired now in an old white suit, neatly patched and clean as snow, he took Adam down to the beach *cantina* to meet more of Caine's disciples. They sat in the warm breeze from a droning fan in a gloomy back room, sipping *café con leche*.

"The *militares* of the poor," Pedro murmured softly. "Your father's small army against *Man First*."

Surprised, he recognized his uncle's shy Negro chauffeur and the grizzled Irish ice-miner he had met on the monorail car from Tycho City. Staggering drunkenly in the gravity of Earth, Thomas O'Toole stood up to shake hands and ordered coffee for them.

The waitress was a blighted redhead. While she went to the kitchen, Pedro murmured that she had been a great beauty from Jalisco and a famous border-town bar-girl. Once, he added, she had been a *novicia* in a convent.

The host was a gaunt scarecrow named Jesus Sabio, a *peon* whose family had been left out, Pedro said, when the government divided the last lands of the old *hacienda*. No Christian, he had once believed in his family legends of the old Aztec gods.

Somehow the news of Caine's coming had brought a stringy-haired girl student in grimy surplus Space Force fatigues on a motor-scooter all the way from California. In search of faith, she had been experimenting with Zen and existentialism and psychochemistry until she heard of Jason Caine.

Somehow, too, the news had brought three shaven-headed human skeletons, scarred and broken from the rigors of some military prison, who had parachuted from an unmarked jet before it crashed into the sea. The Turk had been a Moslem. The Ukranian had been an orthodox Marxist. The Japanese had been a Neo-Buddhist. All of them, before their arrest, had known Solomon Smith at the contact project on the moon.

Except for Pedro and perhaps the Turk, most of them, it seemed to Adam, were broken social outcasts, too poor of body and spirit to stand for an instant against Masters and the tripus. As he sipped his coffee, however, and heard their talk of his father and the glorious hope of trans-galactic contact, he began to feel in them the same luminous devotion he had seen in the black Swan's eyes. He began to catch their faith in Jason Caine.

Later, Pedro made a bed for him in the shed where the fisherman stowed their gear, but he felt no need of rest. He went anxiously back to his father's room, but the Swan said that he was sleeping. Toward sunset he took an impatient walk on the beach, trying in vain to imagine how these shattered men and women were to bring the transgalactic culture to Earth.

At dusk they gathered at a long table in the *cantina* to wait for the inspector. The faded redhead began serving a supper of boiled fish and corn *tortillas,* though the seats at the head of the table were empty. Jason Caine came stooped and stumbling into the dim-lit room, leaning on the black Swan's arm. He stood swaying at his place, gripping the back of his chair.

"I greet you with joy tonight, for you have trusted me." His pain-thinned voice was slow but clear in the breathless hush. "I greet you with sadness, because we may not meet again. Our inspector has arrived, with news for us."

He turned unsteadily toward the dark doorway. Adam's breath caught when Solomon Smith appeared there, with Polly Ming on his arm.

"You all know Smith." Caine smiled fondly at the gangling man in the grime-splotched coveralls. "He was my first follower, and he has been a good student of the cosmic culture. He has served us all."

Smith stood grinning self-consciously with half his face.

"Some of you have met the inspector." Clutching the chair, Caine made an oddly formal little bow toward the girl in the sleek blue sheath. "You know her as Miss Ming."

Adam dropped his fork and almost overturned his chair. He shook his head, scarcely able to believe that Polly could be the alien being who had infiltrated *Man First* to discover the plot to kill his father.

". . . not a human being." Adam caught his father's forced, unsteady voice. "But her devotion to the good of mankind has been more than human."

"How sweet of you, Jason!"

Impulsively, she threw her ivory arms around him and kissed his red-streaked lips. Her face was quivering with emotion when she looked back down the table, and Adam knew the tears in her long eyes were real. Staring dazedly at the flow of rainbows in her sleek dark hair, remembering the excitement of her body in his own arms, he refused to believe she was not a human being.

"Contact is our mission," she said. "All we are doing is only our job."

"Miss Ming is the leader of the transgalactic contact team." Caine's rusty voice quavered out again. "She has come tonight to decide whether or not contact can be opened. I believe it will be—it must be!"

"*Por los pobres!*" Pedro's gentle voice rose pleadingly. "For the miserable ones. For all without work or food or faith."

"I see the need, *Pedrocito.*" She smiled at him tenderly. "But there are rules we must consider. The conditions of contact."

"Before we come to that—" Swaying behind the chair, Caine paused to get his breath. "Miss Ming has brought ugly news. She infiltrated *Man First*, and learned the true cause of my sickness."

The knobby Adam's apple rose and fell in Caine's gaunt throat.

"My sickness is not—not natural." His hoarse voice quivered. "Our friends had protected me from the germs of Earth—from most known dangers."

His fever-glazed eyes stared at his stunned disciples.

"There is a Judas among you!" he whispered harshly. "One of you has sold out to *Man First*. I am dying from a synthetic virus, designed and injected to kill me."

"*Por Dios!*" Pedros moaned. "It cannot be!"

"We had not expected this from one of you." Polly's face was an ivory mask of sorrow beneath the flowing glory of her hair. "But this is true. What I learned did not identify the Judas, but one of you has murdered Jason Caine."

VII

THE FAN DRONED through the hot, accusing quiet. Somewhere out in the *caserío*, a rooster crowed three times. The jaded Jaliscan threw her apron over her ravaged face and fell wailing at Caine's feet.

"One of us a Judas?" the bare-skulled Turk growled thickly. "Allah be merciful!"

The black Swan had helped Caine into his chair. He swayed weakly forward, resting on his elbows, searching the circle of stricken faces with glazed and burning eyes.

"I know you have not yet leared the transgalactic culture," his broken whisper rasped. "I know you cannot help the things you do. I try to understand what one of you has done to me. I try to forgive. But it is hard, hard!"

Nobody looked at anybody else.

"Skin me!" A flash of hope in his greenish eyes, Solomon Smith turned suddenly to Polly Ming. "With all your cosmic science, can't you cure him? Now that you know what this hairy sickness is!"

"We have failed." The exotic Eastern accent had vanished, leaving her voice cool and bright as the clink of pebbles in a stream. "The virus was cleverly tailored to match a stolen sample of Caine's own blood, so that he has no immunity. So far we cannot kill the virus without killing him. If we had more time—"

"We have no time," Caine's harsh whisper interrupted her. "Shall we get on with the question of contact?"

"That is our business tonight." Sadly, slowly, her long eyes swept the circle. "I suppose there is a spy among us, but our decision will be no secret anyhow."

With an unexpected courtliness, Solomon Smith seated her at the head of the table and sat down at her left. The Jaliscan was still whimpering through her greasy apron, but Jesus Sabio came bowing with dishes for them. As deftly as Pedro, Polly folded her *tortilla* to make a spoon for her *frijoles*.

"You understand the conditions." Her lilting voice held a cool assurance now. "To open contact, we must have the agreement of two teams. The human team was Jason Caine and Tom Jett. Contact has been delayed because they failed to agree."

"But Jett ain't playing fair," Smith put in. "Not when he sends his skinnish killers after Jason."

"True." She nodded beneath a halo of rainbows. "Jett has disqualified himself—the spy must tell him that!" Her limpid eyes moved down the table, from Smith to Adam himself. "He has violated the conditions of contact."

Adam flushed before her probing gaze. She looked tantalizingly human. Knowing that she was not, hearing the ring of sure authority in her voice, he felt a chill of awe.

"The virus is a violation because it is an artifact from the outside culture." Her grave eyes returned to Jason Caine. "At the *Man First* Headquarters, I observed other violations. Perhaps Jett failed to realize that his own clandestine misuse of ideas and artifacts from the external culture would have to be interpreted as a sanction of contact."

Jason Caine sat up eagerly.

"You approve?" he gasped. "That is your decision?"

"Not yet." Judicially, she shook her head. "We must not hasten such a critical decision. I am going to review all the evidence and consult with the other members of my team. But don't misunderstand."

She smiled tenderly at Caine.

"I anticipate a favorable decision."

Caine had tasted nothing. At the end of the meal, he stood up unsteadily, leaning on the black Swan.

"A bad time," he gasped. "Hadn't expected this. Hate to say goodbye. Don't know who's the Judas. Whom to trust. Except my son. I do trust Adam."

He stared glassily at Adam.

"My son—" He coughed into his napkin, and Adam saw a spatter of red foam. "My son, I leave my place to you. Guard my people from the Judas. Beat Tom Jett. Open the contact. Open the contact—"

He turned suddenly, coughing again.

"I will, sir!" Adam stood up, choked trembling. "I will—Father!"

He tried to follow, but the black Swan shook her head. "Please. Your father must rest."

She hurried Caine away.

"Come, Adam." Polly Ming had caught his hand. "I must talk to you."

She waited for Solomon Smith and led them out into the warm night. Except for the red flicker of a buzzing neon

100

sign, Vinos Y Cervezas, the *caserío* was dark. At the bottom of the street, Smith unlocked Pedro's fishing shed. Adam gasped at a pile of torn nets and splintered oars and broken engine parts—and the stubby little landing craft, floating above them, glowing dimly green.

She murmured something to Smith. He slipped into the cockpit and pulled the bubble down. Something hummed very faintly. The square craft turned transparent, so that they could see the coils of rope and rusting oil drums piled beyond it. Smith grinned and waved, and then he was gone.

Adam walked up the beach with Polly Ming. The sea was ink-black, but breaking waves splashed the coral with ghostly fire. He clung hard to her hand—to his image of her tender, warm humanity. Yet the fiery tropic stars reminded him coldly that Earth was not her home.

They walked on without speaking until the neon flicker and the loom of the palms were lost behind them. He wanted to ask what she saw when she looked up at the stars, what she recalled, what she felt. But such questions could seem silly. The stars were her world, and this was his.

"I'm afraid, Polly!" he whispered suddenly. "I don't understand anything. I'm terribly afraid."

She stopped and kissed him then, as soundly as any human girl could do.

"You ought to be afraid," she said. "Things won't be easy for you."

"Who is the Judas?" He didn't want to talk about contact; he wanted to forget everything except the human side of Polly Ming. But he couldn't shake that black riddle from his mind. "Is there any evidence?"

"The facts eliminate most of your father's disciples." She spoke now in the brisk official tones of the transgalactic inspector. "The assassin must have been in touch with *Man First*, to receive his equipment and instructions. He must have reached your father, to administer the virus—it was probably injected with an anesthetic jet, though your father was not aware of the shot."

"So that rules out anyone who wasn't on the moon?"

"Exactly." Even under the starlight her hair reflected magic glints, but her voice was crisply impersonal. "The Turk and his friends were safe in prison. The student was on her campus. Pedro and Chino were fishing every day. Jesus and Maria never left the *cantina*. Four suspects are left."

"Four?" Adam was walking close beside her on the crunching coral, clutching her vibrant human hand, but something struck him with a pang of dread. "Four?"

"The Swan," she said. "But I think we can eliminate the Swan. Her race makes her an unlikely *Man First* agent. Watching her tonight, I feel certain she isn't killing your father."

"Thomas O'Toole?"

"O'Toole was on the moon," she said. "Though he wasn't staying at the Tycho Hilton, he did meet your father in the lobby at about the time the virus must have been injected. However, we can't establish any connection with *Man First*. I think O'Toole can be eliminated."

"I'm glad of that," Adam said. "I like O'Toole. But that means—" His breath stopped. "It couldn't be Solomon Smith!"

"Smith was also on the moon," she said. "Your father picked him up from that crater-crawler, along with the audio log. Smith seems to have made a poor record at Project Lifeline."

"He'd lost his rank," Adam said. "He'd been running a private still and drinking too much. He was deserting from the project." He hesitated. "But I like the man," he whispered. "And he was my father's first disciple. I can't believe he did it."

"Probably he didn't." Walking hand and hand with Adam, she kicked at a phosphorescent shell. "Your father had felt no symptoms of the virus at the time he went to pick Smith up. Yet, considering our best estimates of the incubation period, I think the virus must have been injected at least twenty-four hours earlier. I think we can eliminate Smith."

Adam stopped, numb and shuddering, as if the cool sea breeze had chilled him through.

"That leaves—"

His voice dried up.

"You." Her tone was oddly soft. "Adam, that leaves you."

"No!" He dropped her hand and stumbled back. "You can't believe I'm killing my own father."

"General Monk is a *Man First* agent." Once more her tone was briskly formal. "You were with him in a debugged room before you left the Earth. You were with your father in the Tycho Hilton centrifuge at about the time the virus must have been injected. We have reasons for eliminating everybody else."

The soft hiss and muffled rumble of the surf became a wild roaring. The hard beach pitched beneath him. The odors of damp coral and decaying weed became a choking stench of death.

"But—there's something you forget!" He caught frantically at one thread of hope. "You said *Man First* stole a sample of my father's blood, to make the virus. I wasn't on the moon in time to do that."

"We've investigated everything." Her voice was smooth music, cool as the sea wind. "Your father visited the Tycho blood bank a month ago to replace a half-liter of blood for an injured ice-miner. His blood was never used, but it has disappeared from the bank. It must have been stolen by another agent."

"I did not—" His voice shook and broke. "I did not inject that virus in my father!"

"We don't expect you to recall what you have done." She shrugged in the starlight, phantom fireflies dancing in her hair. "*Man First* can control behavior and erase memory with illicit psychodrugs that Jett has imported—that's perhaps his gravest violation of the conditions of contact. Honest or not, your denial means nothing at all."

"They gave me no drugs—"

He choked and stopped, recalling a blinding reek of plastic glue. The soft sea wind became a numbing blizzard. For a moment he couldn't breathe.

"They did!" he gasped. "They did. I was drugged."

He stood trembling in the starlight.

"Help me! Help me, Polly." He reached out imploringly. "I'm so terribly bewildered and afraid. I guess—I guess I just can't realize what is happening to us."

She caught both his hands.

"We'll help you if we can," she murmured soothingly. "We know that cultural contact is often distressing and sometimes destructive—that is why we're here. But the conditions limit what we can do. Any kind of action must wait for our team decision. Now I want to be alone, to consider that."

She gave him a quick cool kiss.

"Go back," she said. "You need rest."

"Oh, Polly! Please—"

She pushed him firmly away and walked on along the beach. He stared blankly after the small shadow of her form and the glow of her hair until she was lost in the dark. Woodenly, then, he plodded back toward the *caserío*.

What to feel—

What to believe—

What to do—

Dazedly, he clutched at desperate bits of evidence to convince himself that he had not brought the virus to kill his father. But every clue dissolved before he touched it. If *Man First* had altered his motives and his memories— the thought was dark madness.

Despairingly, he wondered how he could obey his father's injunctions. To guard the forlorn little band from the Judas— from himself! To beat Tom Jett—with what miracle? To open the transgalactic contact—and plunge his whole world into painful, unforeseeable crisis?

Achingly, he yearned to love and trust and possess Polly Ming. Her tawny enchantment excited him as no girl ever had, not even Kayren Hunter. Yet, human as she seemed, her world was not the Earth. For all her rich compassion, he could never be better than savage or animal to her.

He found himself back at the *caserío*, standing in the doorway of Pedro's fishing shed, where he was to sleep. But those dark specters of dreadful doubt still dogged him. He knew he couldn't sleep. He shook his head and clenched his baffled hands and stumbled back up the beach.

The moon was rising out of the sea. Its waning face looked white and cold. Around behind it, he supposed, General Kalinin was still beaming his signals toward the stars and pondering the Rosetta stone and that colony of ants. He walked on aimlessly, grappling with his own hard problems, until he heard Polly calling.

For a few wild seconds, he imagined that she was calling him. Pulses hammering, his head full of insane conjectures, he ran desperately down the white coral toward the moon until he saw her. He knew then that she was not calling him.

She stood naked on a great black rock, a moonlit dazzle of spray surging all around her. Silver arms lifted, she faced the moon and the molten sea. With a great golden voice, she sang words or tones he had never heard. Her dark hair looked actually luminous, pulsing with pale fire and flowing loose in the sea wind—or was it moving of itself? The sight and sound of her shook him with a frightened excitement.

He stopped abruptly. He knew that he was violating her privacy, and a sense of shame moved him to depart. He walked away a dozen yards, until he thought he heard a different, deeper voice answering her call. He looked back then, and crouched behind a low drift of coral sand.

Something large and faintly luminous was floating in the sea below her rock. Its glistening wet bulge was ridged and dully green. It was shaped, he thought, a little like a huge pineapple. At the top of it was a crown of dancing, golden flame. The deliberate deep reverberation of that other voice came booming from the flame.

With a shock, he realized that this must be another member of the contact team—the philosophic creature that his father called the captain. Trembling with his breathless fascination, sweating now with a fear of discovery, he crouched lower behind the bar of sand.

Strange sound pealed again from the girl's golden throat,

and a little blue cloud lifted out of the moon-glancing water. A queerly coherent puff of luminous smoke, it swooped to the rock and wheeled once around her. It hung still above a pinnacle of rock. A thin stream of bright particles showered down from it to form a small black solid on the rock. The whole bright cloud poured itself out, condensing into a sleek-faced tetrahedron that grew half as tall as Polly.

The first mate, he thought. She must be gathering her team to consider the issue of contact. A fresh terror took his breath. If he were discovered now, his intrusion might prejudice their decison. But he had waited too long to leave. He flattened himself into the damp sand.

He heard a drowsy humming, and saw a glittering swarm rising out of the molten silver beneath the moon. A swirl and twinkle of great, lazy, shining flakes. The swarm divided into three. Bright white bees buzzed around the black pyramid. Huge white moths whined around the captain's golden flame. Droning white fireflies snared themselves in the shimmering net of Polly's hair.

The second mate—

A shift of the cool sea wind brought a strange scent to him. Jungle-rank, yet sweet as honeysuckle, the hot odor recalled a black fragment of his own childhood—a nightmare episode he had never wanted to remember.

He must have been no more than three, because he was in his upstairs bedroom in the rented house in Westmark Manor, where they had moved from his Aunt Victoria's home in the old family mansion.

A slamming door had awakened him. A sudden dark nightwind was blowing through his room, smelling of rain and the honeysuckle his mother had transplanted under his window. He heard thunder grumbling and strange voices crying somewhere in the dark.

He wanted somebody to come and shut his window. The blowing curtains made ghostly shapes when the lightning flickered, and the damp wind felt cold, and he wanted his old room with all his old toys, just across the hall from his Aunt Victoria.

He didn't like thunder in the dark, and he didn't like

the rented house where he was not to damage anything, and he didn't want Joseph Runescribe for his father. Afraid in the dark, he wanted his mother all for himself.

He slipped out of bed and felt his way down the unfamiliar hall to their bedroom door. In the glow of a clock, he saw them naked and fighting on the bed. The hideous little man was on her, panting like an animal. His mother was shuddering and moaning in agony.

Yet she didn't try to get away.

That was the nightmare part. She fought back like another savage animal—and she loved the fighting. He lay terrified behind a chair, afraid to move or breathe, afraid of the gasping violence in Joseph and this beastly madness in his mother, horribly afraid they might find him.

A shutter bang and the thunder was closer and the hot, honeysuckle scent grew strong in the room—always, afterward, he had hated honeysuckle without knowing why. He got cold, and his cramped body ached, and he didn't dare to cry. And still he couldn't understand his mother.

He didn't remember any outcome. Perhaps he had just gone to sleep there on the floor. But he knew now that he had never quite trusted his mother after that night. Nor any woman, not entirely. Expecting betrayal from the best of them, he had behaved accordingly. It struck him painfully that he had not been fair to Kayren Hunter, when he dropped her so suddenly. Or even to the black Swan, when he dated her on the moon.

Lying sweating and shivering on the wet sand, he watched the whirling, singing, gleaming bees and moths and white fireflies—that were not bees or moths or fireflies at all. He watched the spray-drenched captain bobbing closer to the rock. He watched the tiny plumes of bright blue smoke that spurted from the black points of the first mate to ring the white moths in small blue halos. He watched Polly dancing with the fireflies in her hair, and he felt a stabbing ache of rejected loneliness.

Apprehensively, he waited for the third mate—for the fighting sonneteer that had given Caine the shakes. But it did not come. He decided that it must have stayed with the starship, to protect this odd shore excursion from greater dangers than a frightened man behind a drift of sand.

But something else did come out of the tossing spray. A tapered greenish whip lashed up across the black north face of the rock, searched swiftly for a grasp, secured itself in a fissure, thickened with a quick contraction.

He flattened himself into the sand, still numb and shuddering with that secret terror that had lain hidden in him since he was three years old. The thing must be a giant octopus—that was his first shocked thought. But in a moment he knew that it was something out of space.

The tripus!

Had Jett sent the tripus to kill the contact team? That shocking fear crushed his chest and cut his limbs to mincemeat. He tried to scream a warning, but fear had clogged his throat with bitter dust. He could only gasp and stare.

But it was not the tripus.

It was shapeless, flowing from the moon-white water like a monstrous amoeba. Darker than the foam, it glowed dully green. Two buried eyes, vague spots of baleful red deep beneath its translucent slime, were fixed on Polly Ming.

If not the tripus, it must be yet another creature of Tom Jett's. Another violation of the conditions of contact, something a little more dreadful than the black genifacts and the virus in his father's blood. He thought it must have slipped past the third mate's watch.

He tried again to shout a warning, but recollection had broken a dam in his mind. A cold tide of paralyzing dread swept him back to the floor of that rented house in Westmark Manor, that night when he was three.

He lay frozen, cramped and sick and breathless, watching the invader climb the slick wet rock. New limbs whipped out of it, groped for grasping places, hauled it upward terribly fast. Flowing like living lava beneath its slimy crust, it had no shape, yet its baleful buried eyes never left Polly Ming.

He gasped with relief when the bees and moths and fireflies discovered it. The swarmed above it, whining like angry silver hornets. They streamed back to the golden flame and the black pyramid and the girl's glowing hair, but their warning came too late.

A thin green whip caught Polly's ankle.

She screamed and struggled then. The bees and moths left the captain and the first mate. They swirled up with the white fireflies around her, all furious hornets now, darting in as if to sting that hideous blob of crawling jelly.

But all they did was useless. Thin cruel coils caught her golden arms, dragged her shrieking toward the monstrous eyes inside that heaving, flowing, fearful mass.

At last his desperation broke the barriers of fear. Sweating and gasping, he staggered stiffly to his feet. Groping wildly for any weapon, he tore his fingers on a coral mass too big for him to move, kicked at a dark heap that was only rotting weed, snatched a heavy stick of driftwood out of the sand.

Limping on his stiffened legs, he ran down the beach and splashed toward the rock. The hornets came swarming to meet him. Strange, frail silver flakes spun like dry leaves in a whirlwind. Their high whine became a tiny voice crying, *Stay away! Stay away!*

He tried to climb the rock. His fingers slipped in the foul green slime the creature had left. He fell back into a breaking wave. Roaring water dragged him down, filled his nose and mouth with sand, battered him against the jagged rock.

He came up again, blowing brine and clinging to his club. The silver hornets found him again, whining, *Go away! Go away!* But he lurched and slipped and stumbled up the rock.

Now the hornets were a cloud around his head. They stung his cheeks and fluttered in his eyes and got tangled in his hair. Their soft bright wings had a hot, musky scent, oddly like the reek of the slippery slime on the rock. They clung around his ears, sighing, *Get away! Get away!*

Ducking away from them, skidding on the slime, he came to the top of the rock. That great shapeless shape had swallowed Polly. Her long body was a pale shadow in it, dim in the glare of the buried eyes. Only her agonized face was left outside, and a luminous wisp of her hair, and her tawny hand clutching a last shrinking coil.

Frantic, he lifted his club to strike—

Get away! the tiny, whining hornets cried. *Go away! Stay away!*

He swung the salt-soaked timber with all his strength toward the nearest glaring eye. The hornets hushed and scattered. Almost too quick for him to see it, a live green rope snatched the club and whipped around his body and tossed him off the rock.

The high moon was in his eyes, when he came to. He was cold and stiff and bruised. He lay face up on the rough coral, his clothing wet and full of gritty sand. He moaned and sat up painfully.

The receding tide had left a litter of dark weed and scattered puddles of black water around the rock, but the captain and the mates and the attacker were gone. He shivered in the cold wind from the moonlit sea, wondering if the whole event had been some kind of drugged nightmare.

"Adam!"

Polly's soft call startled him. Lurching rustily to his feet, he found the stubby little landing craft hovering a dozen yards behind him. Solomon Smith was opening the bubble. Polly Ming slipped out of the cockpit and ran barefoot to him.

He stared at her unbelievingly, because she showed no mark of the assault he recalled. Beneath a wisp of filmy nightwear, she looked pink and clean and radiant. Her quick smile was tender and innocently quizzical.

"The engineer wants to apologize," she said. "He assumed that you were attacking us under *Man First* control, and I'm afraid he was pretty tough with you."

"The engineer?" He felt blank. "Who's the engineer?"

"He's with the contact team," she said. "We haven't let many human beings meet him, because we knew the response would be negative—"

"That slimy monster—" His jaw sagged. "Do you mean it wasn't hurting you?"

Her dark head shook demurely.

"Your quaint system of taboos makes the affair awkward to explain." Her voice was smoothly soothing, but her long eyes had a glint of secret amusement. "You must remember that I'm not human."

"I—I ought to know," he muttered huskily. "But you look so damned human!"

"Thank you, Adam!" Her smile took his breath. "I was chosen to lead the team because of certain traits that do show a high quotient of human appeal. But now you must understand that in most respects we aren't at all human-like."

He swayed giddily, too deeply disturbed to say anything.

"Our race has evolved sex in a way that may seem quaint to you," she said. "We not only have more sexual types than you do, but members of each type can pass through several sexual phases. I am still very young. Someday, when I'm ready to leave this human-like phase, I'll metamorphose. My matured body cells will disassociate, to enter a different way of life. In that next phase, I'll be like the person Caine calls the first mate."

"That queer cloud?" Adam stared at the empty rock, and back into the innocent enchantment of her heart-shaped face. "The shining smoke that settled into that black pyramid?" The night wind was icy on the back of his neck. "You'll turn to *that*?"

"If you expect to find human creatures and human customs on every world there is, you might as well stay at home." Her demure eyes twinkled at his dazed dismay. "Later," she added more gravely, "I may change again —if I am ever wise enough—into something like the person Caine calls the captain."

"The engineer—" He lost his voice. "The engineer—"

"You will have to understand that we are all one family." She was gentle as a flower petal, fresh and pure as spring. "No other arrangement would be endurable, on a mission that takes so long as ours. You'll have to understand that all the others are what I suppose you'd have to call my husbands."

He dropped his face and staggered backward. His skin felt hot with a flush of shame. Vaguely, now, he remembered his mother's stupid efforts to explain when she had found him sleeping on the floor after that hateful night when he was three.

A heaving sickness choked him.

"Don't feel bad about it," Polly was urging him brightly. "We all know you didn't understand. The engineer was perfectly able to protect us both, so no harm was done. Really, dear, you mustn't feel so bad."

He did feel bad—ashamed and angry and vaguely afraid. Yet, when he raised his eyes to her tender ivory face, her high quotient of appeal struck him like a surge of madness. All at the same instant, he wanted to slap her and kiss her and run away from her.

All he did was try to gulp his sickness down.

". . . hazard of contact." The soothing music of her voice seemed more remote than the cold moon. "People always find that much of what they had taken for basic truth is either trivial or false. The real trouble comes because they tend to abandon all their values, even those they ought to keep. For that reason it is sometimes wise for a new people to delay contact."

He wondered dully what her team had decided about opening the Earth to contact, but he thought he couldn't stand to talk about it now. Giving up his own basic truths was still as hard as it had been when he was three.

Suddenly he burst into tears.

"My darling man!" Her voice held an instant warm solicitude. "You're worn completely out. We must get you back to the *caserío*."

She beckoned to Solomon Smith, and the landing craft came skimming down the beach. Smith's unshaven face held a knowing grin that made him flush again. He climbed stiffly into the cockpit, and they took him back to Pedro's fishing shed.

"Sleep." She kissed his forehead lightly. "You'll feel better."

He hung his sea-soaked clothing over the oil drums to dry, and went to sleep on the bed of palm leaves and old sails that Pedro had made for him. He did sleep. Perhaps he felt better. But Chino woke him at dawn to tell him his father was dead.

He stumbled through the cool half-light to find the flat dead husk on the pallet, covered with a threadbare blanket. The tired black Swan bent over the shrunken head, wiping the blood-clotted mouth and closing the glassy eyes. He stood watching miserably, knowing nothing to do.

The other disciples came shuffling and whispering after him into the hushed adobe room. The haggard Jaliscan knelt beside the Swan, crooning dolefully. Jesus Sabio had been a barber; he would wash and shave the body. Pedro had carpenter tools; he would make the coffin in his shed. Chino would ride the motor scooter to the *municipio*, to inform the police.

"*El padre, también?*"

That question caused a whispered argument. Without the blessing of a priest, Jesus pointed out, he could not be buried at the old mission above the *caserío*. Pedro objected that his faith had not been in that old church of crumbling stone, but in the transgalactic culture, which would bring eternal life and peace and joy to this Earthly world. The hysterical Jaliscan wailed that he had earned a decent Christian burial. But Caine had not been merely a Christian, the Turk protested. All religion was a symbolic statement of man's moral wisdom, the Neo-Buddhist agreed, and no transgalactic contact would destroy true religion—

"Skin it!" Smith's nasal voice interrupted the debate. "Caine ain't got no papers. He ain't legally here—no more than most of the rest of us. Call the local cops—and what happens? They investigate the hide off us."

He peered around the dusky room.

"In spite of the hairy Judas, I don't think *Man First* knows where we are. If they did, they'd do more about it. Maybe let a military jet crash on the *caserío* with a live

113

bomb aboard. Let's slip his body out, just like we slipped him in."

The Jaliscan began sobbing again that *el Contactor* must have a proper funeral, but she stopped at some murmured word from the Swan. Smith came quietly across the room to Adam.

"The team advises this," he said. "If you don't object."

Adam looked at the pallet and swallowed hard and shook his head. Pedro and Chino made a stretcher of two poles and a torn sail. Smith helped them lift it into the cockpit of the landing craft, and the black Swan went with the body.

He was drinking bitter coffee in the *cantina*, sitting silent at a little table with the despondent Turk and the brooding Irishman, when Smith returned. Polly Ming came with him. Though she had changed to a plain dress less revealing than her gauzy nightwear, her tawny body still displayed a shattering quotient of appeal.

She sat with them. Jesus Sabio brought coffee to the table. Pedro and Chino came to stand respectfully behind her chair. When she looked at Adam, he thought he saw a glow of compassion in her long limpid eyes, but when she spoke he flinched from the cool authority of her smooth official voice.

"In communion, our team has come to a decision. This was a hard decision, because we anticipate that the readjustments of contact will be painful for most human beings. Technological progress is too far ahead of moral maturity here. Some of us had grave doubts that Earth is ready for contact."

She paused, and Adam felt a hot surge of irrational annoyance at the clatter of Smith's spoon, stirring sugar into his coffee.

"The crucial factor in our deliberations was Jett's persistent violation of the conditions of contact." Her voice was aloof, melodious, serenely judicial. "On the one hand, the illicit activities of *Man First* are the most distressing evidence of man's moral immaturity. On the other hand, the introduction of external ideas and artifacts has brought the planet to an alarming crisis for which the external culture must at least share responsibility."

When she looked at Smith, he suddenly stopped the irritating clink of his spoon.

"As the best solution to this unpleasant situation, we have ruled that Jett's own violations have disqualified his earlier vote against contact. In fact, immediate contact seems to offer the only hope that Earth can be rescued from the ugly consequences of what Jett has done. Even that is an uncertain hope. But your world is now open to contact."

Adam braced himself to meet her probing eyes.

"As your father wished, Adam Cave, we have selected you for the first effort to implement this contact." The quiet power of her voice left him shivering with awe. "A contact machine is now being prepared for you. I'll take you to it. We all wish you good luck!"

"*Viva!*" Pedro shouted. "*Viva el hijo del Contactor!*"

Adam stood up after the small chorus of *vivas* had died away. Flushed and uncomfortable, he promised that he would do his best for contact. For his father's sake.

He walked back with Smith and Polly to Pedro's shed, where they had left the landing craft. He made her stop beneath a tattered palm while Smith went on.

"If you think I'm a *Man First* spy," he whispered fiercely, "why are you sending me out first? Is it—is it just to dispose of me?"

"Perhaps." She shrugged. "There are many reasons. This is what your father asked for. If we are wrong—if you are really innocent of your father's death and free of Jett's secret power—you have this chance to prove yourself."

"I am innocent—I think I am innocent!" he whispered desperately. "I thank you for the chance."

"Thank Smith," she said. "He has a curious faith in you."

He stared at the gangling man in the greasy coveralls, wondering darkly what the source of that faith might be.

"If we are right—" Her cool voice continued, "if you are still an unconscious creature of *Man First*—then it is wise

115

to remove you in this way from the group of Caine's disciples. You cannot play Judas again."

With no reply, he could only bend his head.

"In any case," she added almost casually, "your reception should give us a better idea of the capabilities of *Man First*. Jett has been preparing to defend the Earth from contact. We need to know what his preparations are."

"I see!" Adam whispered bitterly. "You mean I'm expendable!"

"We are all of us expendable," she agreed sweetly. "But you are the most expendable man."

VIII

ADAM SPENT ONE more night on the pile of palm leaves and mildewed sails in the fishing shed, troubled by nightmares in which the transgalactic engineer pursued him reproachfully through honeysuckle jungles, thrusting at him with a green, slime-crusted whip, wanting to shake hands.

Chino awakened him at daybreak.

"*La virgen* ees arrive!" His black Chinese face was eagerly aglow. "The miraculous *virgen del contacto*. She take you to *la máquina*."

Still disturbed by his dreams of the engineer, Adam reflected that "virgin" was an odd word for Polly Ming. Yet, when they found her hovering in the landing craft under the molting palms, she looked as dewily immaculate as any merely human virgin. She opened the bubble for him.

"*Viva!*" Chino waved him into the cockpit. "*Viva el macho! Viva el hijo del Contactor.*"

Polly greeted him with a more-than-human poise and charm.

"You are a hero now. Your planting of the transgalactic

culture is a great moment for your race." Somehow the smooth music of her voice reminded him that the moment was not so great for hers. "For your planet, it's the beginning of something like a birth. The age of quiet and lonely growth is ended. Earth will be born into a greater world, with room for more splendid achievement—and sometimes more painful defeat."

The palms dimmed and flickered as she touched the panel. The pale dawn dissolved into a denser dark.

"It's illogical!" Adam burst out. "Preposterous! How can you send me to plant a culture I know nothing about?"

"We didn't plan it this way."

Demurely grave in the greenish glow of the panel, she shrugged entrancingly. "We gave your contact team many years of transgalactic travel and special education. But your father is dead and Tom Jett is against us. You'll have to do the best you can."

Her devastating perfume filled the small cockpit.

"Actually, the machine itself will be the cultural reservoir. The conditions of contact require it to be commanded by a native human being, but you will be responsible only for decisions of general policy. Once the routine is set up, the machine can carry it out."

He sat far from her, trying hard to resist her irresistible quotient of appeal.

"You're to begin at Westmark." Her voice was brightly calm, almost casual. "Your old home town. If you can plant the new culture there, against the opposition of the Monks and *Man First*, there shouldn't be much trouble anywhere else."

The egg-shaped contact machine was floating low in a rough sea when they found it, a wide dome of bright golden metal with white spray flying over it. The sun looked two or three hours high when he saw it through the scudding clouds; he guessed they had come two or three thousand miles east, to somewhere in the Atlantic.

A broad panel folded down toward the tossing waves to make a dock, and Solomon Smith ran out across it to meet them—looking doll-sized in his spotted coveralls until Adam realized the immensity of the dome. Polly dropped the landing craft beside him on the stage.

"Courage, Adam!" She lifted her elfin ivory face, long eyes half closed, and he kissed her in spite of himself. "If you have questions, just ask the machine."

The bubble opened. He stepped uncertainly down to the dock. Watching Smith scramble into the cockpit with Polly, watching her warm kiss of greeting, he felt unreasonably hurt and forlorn.

"What now?" he demanded desperately. "What do I do now?"

"Skin!" Smith gave him a lazy, lopsided grin. "Just ask the machine."

"Huh?"

Smith closed the bubble. Polly snuggled up to him as eagerly as if he had been another transgalactic engineer. They both waved gaily at Adam. Their little craft whined faintly. They flickered and blurred and were gone.

Alone on the dock, Adam leaned against a sudden booming gust of wind. A leaping wave shattered against the golden curve beneath him, and cold spray spattered him. He stumbled toward the edge of the unrailed stage.

Cold panic caught him. Events were pushing him too fast, like some wild torrent sweeping him toward the roar of an unknown waterfall. Peering frantically for a way out, he could see nothing anywhere except white-capped seas and scudding clouds. He felt very small and very much alone.

Greetings, Adam Cave.

The voice came out of the dark dome behind him. Oddly quiet, it was yet oddly penetrating, as if no other sound could keep it from him. Inhumanly precise, it yet somehow reflected the warm human tones of Polly Ming, as if it had learned English from her.

Welcome to your new post as commander of Contact Machine Earth One. Do you wish to enter the machine and give us your orders?

Without much choice, he walked as calmly as he could across the wide stage and into the dome. Promptly, the stage folded upward behind him. He found himself shut inside a wide gallery that ringed the dome. Transparent from within, the outer wall gave him a golden-tinted view of sun and clouds and heaving sea.

What are your instructions?

He looked around uncertainly, but the voice came from no source that he could see. The inner wall of the gallery was a shining curve of golden metal. He walked around it until the sun came back into view.

"Who—who are you?" He stopped and gulped, trying to smooth his own creaky voice. "Where are you?"

We are the first contact machine on your Earth. Unlike his own, the voice made no echo in the gallery; perhaps it came to him by something more subtle than sound. *We are now floating in the North Atlantic, ready to plant the transgalactic culture in the city of Westmark, under your direction. Shall we proceed?*

He caught his breath and braced himself.

"Proceed!"

The gray Atlantic faded. A tide of empty blackness rose outside the gallery, but the golden walls inside shone faintly. Resolutely cool, Adam walked slowly around the endless curve of the dome, until the darkness glowed with another dawn. Against the red-streaked eastward sky, he recognized the squat bulk of the Monk building and the clustered skyscrapers of downtown Westmark.

We are now at the center of Monk Park in Westmark, the machine said. *Shall we proceed?*

"Proceed."

Watching from the gallery, he waited uncomfortably. Though the great golden egg was not yet quite real, he had known Monk Park since his Aunt Victoria used to take him riding there in her quiet electric gold cart when he could first remember.

Named for old Abraham Monk, founder of her family and the city itself, the park was a wooded square-mile just west of the main business district. The once-exclusive residential sections around it had long ago decayed, and it was now a perilous border territory between the Negro ghetto on the north and the Latin-American quarter on the south and the native white slums west across the river.

On the gallery, he stood perhaps a hundred feet above the park. At first it lay empty in the smoggy dawn, a neglected jungle laced with rubbish-cluttered roads. He stood for a moment wondering blankly what the transgalactic culture would mean to the juvenile gangs who prowled here.

Two newsboys on bicycles came around a clump of trees. They saw the machine. Staring, they ran together and fell, scattering rolled papers. For a moment they stood gazing. Then they were pedaling furiously away.

A little later he began to hear the surging murmur of wonder. The grimy old apartment buildings that walled the park were so far away that individual voices or figures were hard to make out, but an awed buzz floated over the trees, and the swarms of staring people made dark clots on fire escapes and balconies and roofs. They were more than half a mile away.

"What happens now?" he muttered huskily. "Exactly how do we bring them the transgalactic culture?"

We have begun, the machine said. *We are using all radio and television channels to establish contact. Do you wish to monitor our transmissions?*

"I guess—" He caught his breath. "I do!"

"People of Westmark—"

Startled to hear the warm, soft voice of Polly Ming, he spun to find that a section of the golden inner wall had dissolved into a stereo screen. She stood there in pure white, haloed against a dazzle of light behind her head.

"The object you can see in Monk Park is Contact Machine Earth One. The commander is your own fellow townsman, Adam Cave. The machine comes to open your contact with the culture of the galaxies. This is how it looks."

Her appealing image dissolved from the screen. In its place he saw the great golden egg itself, as the frightened boys must have seen it, looming tall as the gray Monk Building. It rested on a cushion of white fire.

"Now we bring you a recorded message from James Cave," her vibrant voice rang on. "The father of Adam Cave, he led the two-man team from Project Lifeline that took the beginning steps toward contact many years ago. He will tell you what the transgalactic culture means to you."

The message must have been recorded before that killing virus was injected. A sharp ache caught Adam's throat when he saw his father smiling from the halo on the screen, ruddy skin and keen blue eyes and flowing yellow hair all bright with their hues of optimism.

"Thank you, Inspector." The kind eyes looked quickly off as if at Polly Ming. "People of Westmark, you have just seen and heard the charming inspector of the transgalactic team—the generous beings who have come across space to share with us their arts and science and philosophy. Now I want to talk to you about contact.

"This contact team has come from an organization I'll call just the Club. The Club is not a government. The team has not come to conquer or to rule or to destroy the old life of Earth, but simply to offer us what we wish to take. Yet some of you will be disturbed."

Adam heard a far screech of sirens when his father paused. Turning to the crystal wall, he saw police cars converging toward him through the park. Down on River Road, which had been empty a few minutes before, he saw a thickening jam of traffic, but the clotted human swarms looked thinner on the roofs and fire escapes of the decayed apartment towers beyond. Toy-small fire trucks were racing through the Negro streets north, and sudden white blooms of tear gas were opening all along the foot of the tenement cliffs.

Somebody, he thought, was already disturbed.

". . . machine is peaceable." Again he heard his father's urgent voice. "It will not attack any human individual or any native institution. Yet, because our lives will all be changed, it is important for each of you to understand the guiding principles of the Club."

Adam heard a far crackle of pistol shots.

"Each human individual is a worthwhile end, not a means to another end," his father said. "That principle is not new on Earth, but contact has brought us a technology that can change it from admirable theory to common practice. The machine has come to set you free."

An explosion somewhere thudded dully.

"The machine brings each one of you freedom from need. Life requires mass and energy and space. Mass converts to energy, however, so that the basic needs of life are only mass and space. On our earth, these are still abundant. The machine brings us the science and the know-how to supply every physical need of every human being."

Somewhere a machine gun stuttered.

"The machine brings you freedom to know—freedom from ignorance and superstition and fear," his father said. "To all who wish to learn, it opens all the knowledge that a billion races have gathered from many billion worlds. Along with this knowledge, it offers you new ways to learn and remember, to think and to speak."

Angry shouts drifted faintly across the park.

"To assure each of you freedom from need and freedom to know," James Cave said, "the machine brings you freedom of action. To all who ask, it offers protection from domineering individuals and coercive institutions. It opens the frontiers and the ghettos and even the prisons."

Adam heard a muffled, distant rumbling.

"Come to the contact machine!" The smiling, vital man in the screen reached out both his eager arms, as if to embrace the world. "The Club offers each of you an individual link—your own personal contact with the transgalactic culture. This link will be a small device coded to your own mind and body so that it cannot be taken from you. Through this link, the Club will bring you the freedoms we have been talking about.

"All these freedoms are free to you.

"We require no payment, now or later. We demand no promises. We exact no taxes. We make no exceptions. We offer all the benefits of contact to everyone who asks, old or young, wise or foolish, sick or well, subject or ruler, just or not."

His father's smile turned wry.

"Cynics among you will question this. They will say

that our offer is a hoax, because nobody would—or could —give so much for nothing. Let me say to them that we do expect something. We know that even the cynics will be changed by contact. Most of you will want to make some return for what you have received. The return we expect is that you will somehow aid our work or perhaps even seek to join the Club—"

The voice stopped. The stereo screen was gone, leaving the curved golden wall apparently unbroken. The firing rattled far away.

Adam Cave—

Out of nowhere, he heard the soundless voice of the machine itself.

Commander Cave, that is the substance of our proclamation to your people. We are still repeating our prepared messages on every possible channel. But the opponents of contact have begun to react against us with great vigor, as you can see for yourself.

Looking out, he saw that the park was empty. The police cars were gone. The traffic jam had disappeared. In its place, an armored column wound along River Road. Splotch-painted turrets spun, swinging long guns toward him.

North and west and south, the walling tenements looked equally empty. The humming human swarms were gone. A few ant-sized men were stacking sandbags around toy guns. A black thread of smoke floated into the sunbright sky from a blazing building in the Mexican section, south.

Man First has taken over the local government and declared military law, the machine said. *General Monk is in command here. His forces are sealing us in, so that the people cannot approach us. He is jamming our signals. His broadcasters are stating that our call is a hoax, planned to cover an invasion from space. They are stating that James Cave is dead.*

A sonic boom jarred him. White fire blazed from the long shadow of the machine. Rocks and trees and dark smoke geysered upward from a wide wound in the Earth. The jet that had brought the missile screamed on, a sun-glinting spark climbing now in the bright sky over River Road.

"Can we defend ourselves?" Adam gasped. "Can we fight back?"

We can use no violence, the machine said. *The conditions of contact, laid down by the Club, forbid the use of force against any man or any human institution.*

"Even against *Man First?*"

Even against Man First.

"Must we let them destroy us?"

They cannot destroy us, the machine answered. *Not with these primitive weapons. When a missile approaches, we simply rotate our mass enough so that it passes through without harm.*

Adam peered down again into that raw crater beneath the thinning plume of smoke. Again he traced the jet's path. He shivered at the probability that the missile had passed through his own body.

"Do they have better weapons?" he inquired uneasily. "Weapons from the worlds outside?"

We compute a high probability that they will soon be able to employ illicit transgalactic weapons, the machine said. *If that happens, our mission has failed. It may fail in any case.*

"Can't we get better weapons?"

We cannot. We are forbidden to import or use weapons of any type. The conditions of contact prohibit war, even to protect the machine itself.

"So time is against us?"

Man First can defeat us, with delay alone, the machine agreed. *Our opponents need not touch us at all. They need no transgalactic weapons. All they must do is keep the people sealed away from contact with us. We must reach the people.*

The machine stopped. For a moment Adam stood listening to the gathering rumble of trucks and tanks and missile launchers and the high scream of a wheeling jet.

In this predicament, the machine demanded, *what are your orders?*

Adam bit his lip.

"We can't quit."

He hesitated uncertainly, peering out across the dirty brown carpet of smog at the sunlit skyscrapers clustered around the square gray mass of the Monk building.

"I'll try to reach the people." He straightened resolutely. "Some of them might listen—some who have influence. My family. Friends. The girl I was going to marry. Can you get a message to Senator Monk?"

We can transmit a message.

The machine transmitted messages.

Man First agrees to a meeting, it presently informed him. *Senator Monk will be unable to attend, but he says a suitable spokesman will be chosen to represent the family and Man First. General Monk has promised to halt military action while the meeting takes place, but he insists that you must come out of the machine.*

"I'll do that," Adam said.

The suggested meeting place is four hundred yards down the road, toward the downtown district, the machine said. *At that point we cannot offer you complete protection. In case of treachery, your life will be in danger.*

"I'll take a chance."

By midmorning, the arrangements were complete. A door opened inside the gallery and a small elevator dropped Adam to ground level. As he stepped out, a device like a vending machine tossed him a four-inch egg of what looked like burnished gold.

Take it with you, the machine told him. *It is an individual contact link. In event of treachery, it will offer you a degree of protection. If you find protection unnecessary you may give it to the Man First spokesman as evidence of our own good faith.*

The little egg felt oddly light and slightly warm. Carrying it in one hand, he walked down the ramp out of the machine. Outside, the ramp bridged a coldly glowing pit. He hurried down across it to the pavement and turned to look back.

The machine loomed huge behind him, a great golden

egg of infinite promise. Its vast curve blazed in the sun, brighter he thought than gold. He stared at what was happening beneath it.

Moving plumes of cold white fire were somehow dissolving the soil and rock around its back. Something veiled in cold bright fog was somehow converting the dissolved mass into new shapes of silvery metal and polished crystal. The same shining plumes were building the gleaming beams and colored crystal bricks into a massive foundation beneath the egg.

"Huh!" Wonder took his breath. "What's going on?"

We are building a contact center for Westmark.

The precise voice came now, he supposed, from the small golden egg in his hand, but it seemed the same, still sourceless and soundless, somehow sent to him alone. It still echoed Polly Ming.

This center will offer the benefits of contact to the people of Westmark, it said. *It will also make new contact machines which you can send to other cities. That is unless our whole mission fails—*

"Our mission must not fail!"

He stood for half a minute, watching long fingers of cold glowing mist lifting a great bright I-beam into place on two ruby piers. The crystal might be quartz purified from sandstone, he thought, and the metal must be aluminum and magnesium refined from clay. Or was the machine transmuting elements?

Man First, however, was the pressing question now. He turned down the winding drive toward the meeting place. The empty park seemed curiously peaceful at first, the neglected grass brown with drought and worn down to clay where children had played. But then he had to pick his way around the smoking rim of a great crater a *Man First* missile had made.

Beyond the underpass, he found the appointed place—a concrete bench where vandals had scrawled and scratched dirty words in three languages. The spokesman for the Monks and *Man First* who came to meet him there was little Joseph Runescribe.

Waving a white handkerchief tied to a walking cane, he darted through the smog-blighted trees at a nervous trot. He came bareheaded, in an out-of-fashion mauve seersucker suit that looked too big in the shoulders and too tight at the belly.

"A distressing situation, Adam!"

He shook hands with a prissy formality that failed to hide his fear. Above the pointed beard, his dark narrow face was sweat-beaded in the humid June heat, and sweat made black circles under his armpits. His strong scent made Adam think first of Polly Ming in the green-slimed embrace of the transgalactic engineer, and then of his mother in Joseph's arms, that night when he was three. In a flash of painful understanding, he saw why he had never quite liked Joseph, and he felt a wave of futile pity for him. Surely a high-minded scholar should have the right to marry a handsome widow without incurring a small boy's hatred.

"Especially distressing—to your poor mother—and to me." Joseph sat puffing on the cracked concrete bench. "Things are going too fast for us. We can't understand that object, or how you got involved with it."

His eyes darted toward the golden glare of the machine.

"A few weeks ago we were so proud of you." His voice was a fretful whine. "You and Kayren had everything. The whole family was so happy for you. Of course you had to throw it all away. But I can't see how things got to this."

"That's what I've come to tell you."

To reassure himself, Adam glanced back at the dome above the dusty trees. It looked immense and real and wonderful. The hot air quivered to the roar of three jets wheeling above it in the sun, but they were not attacking.

"You—everybody has got to understand about contact." He groped for language. "We've got to wake up, Joseph. This machine has come to bring us progress. Progress—unlimited! The greatest wisdom and the best machines from billions of years of progress on billions of different worlds. Ours for free! All we have to do is convince the family and *Man First*—"

"You know I don't believe in progress." Bird-like, Joseph

hopped nervously back to his feet. "But have you considered what this means to your poor mother?" His sharp little eyes darted accusingly at Adam. "We were sitting at breakfast when she saw your father in that canned broadcast. She thought he was still alive. A frightful jolt. I had to put her back to bed, with a double tranquilizer."

"I wish he were alive," Adam whispered bitterly. "Since he's dead, I'm leading the contact team. You've got to listen to me, Joseph. You've got to help me persuade the senator and the bishop and the general—"

"Not likely!" Joseph sniffed. "I've just come from a family shindy in the senator's office. None of them believes this wild tale of universal altruism. They're all convinced that it's a devilish hoax—invented to cover an invasion of the Earth!"

"This will show you it's no hoax."

He held out the little golden egg, and Joseph recoiled as if he thought it was about to hatch a hooded cobra.

"An individual contact link," he said. "The Club will give one like it to every human being who asks. You take this one, Joseph. It's your own private guarantee of all the physical and mental and social benefits my father was talking about. Test it. Show it to the senator and the bishop and the general—"

"Get it away from me!" Joseph cowered from it. "I won't touch it."

But you do need the benefits of contact, Dr. Runescribe.

Joseph cringed away from the sweet soundless voice.

Your physical needs are desperate. A quick examination shows that you are now in pain from a recurrent gastric ulcer.

"How did you know?" He clutched at his belly and blinked at the egg. "How can you tell?"

By analysis of all your body radiations. The ulcer is caused by the general tension of your whole culture. Such cultural conflicts take time to remove, but we can relieve the pain almost at once by local therapy.

"Take it away!" He peered wildly at Adam. "Don't let it touch me."

"As you say," Adam agreed. "That is a fourth freedom which the Club is offering every human being. Besides freedom from need and freedom to know and freedom to act, there is freedom of choice—freedom to reject the galactic culture. Every person must have that freedom."

"Piffle!"

Joseph sat again on the concrete bench. His bright little eyes were fixed on the egg. His hand was still pressed against his belly, and now Adam could see the lines of pain etched into his dark, pointed face.

"Enough of your phony freedoms!" he gasped. "I came here to talk about something else. I want to tell you about the family shindy."

"How is Kayren?" Adam asked impulsively. "Have you seen her?"

"She's still at the senator's office." His thin lips twitched. "But you threw her over, Adam. You hurt her terribly. You'll never get her back."

"I only wanted to know how she is."

"Time's running out." Joseph glanced nervously up at the wheeling jets. "Adam, I've brought a message from the family. We want you to listen to reason. We want you to get that thing out of Westmark—and off the Earth."

He nodded grimly toward the blazing dome.

"If you don't, the general says he'll hit you with everything we've got. That's plenty. You haven't a chance."

"If you're all so sure, why bother talking?" Adam studied his pain-creased face. "Why don't you hit us now?"

"My dear boy!" His shocked look was almost convincing. "Don't you know how much we care for you? Your Aunt Vicky has been begging for your life. You still could have all her millions."

"If I give up," Adam muttered. "But I won't give up. You've got to listen to me—"

"We've been listening all morning to your illegal broadcasts," Joseph broke in harshly. "Now you'll listen to us. Listen to what the bishop said."

Adam listened, probing every word and gesture for evidence of something more than family fondness. Even Aunt

Victoria couldn't care that much. Joseph's sweating unease reflected some secret weakness in the position of *Man First*, if he could only find it.

"The bishop says it's blasphemy." Joseph's nasal whine went high. "He says all your promises of a paradise on Earth are a mockery of the true religion. Even if you could deliver these promised freedoms—which all of us doubt—they're all false values. They're material bribes to lure people away from spiritual truth. If you offer people immortal youth and perfect happiness here on Earth, what will happen to the church? The bishop wants to know."

"I'm not sure he has the true religion." Adam shrugged sardonically. "If he's not worried about the earthly lives of the people here—the Negroes and Mexican and poor whites the police have been chasing off the roofs around the park— I think he ought to worry about his church."

"Watch yourself, my dear boy." Joseph gave him a thin brown scowl. "Religion and the law are our defenses. Attack them, and you destroy the family. But don't think we aren't concerned about the deprived people here."

Joseph reproved him with a bright sparrow blink.

"Just now at the shindy, the senator was fretting about his constituents here. You know this has been a bad year for riots and strikes. We had an ugly strike at the mills, even before that object appeared." His worried eyes darted at the dome.

"The senator was outraged by those canned broadcasts. He says you've brought us ruin. Labor is still restless. Inflation is getting out of hand. Profits were down two percent last year in our family trust. The senator's out of sorts because of something his colored chauffeur said before he disappeared—nobody knows where."

Afraid of betraying his father's followers at the *caserío*, Adam tried not to move his face.

"The senator wants to know what your damned gadgets will do to our economic system." Joseph squinted suspiciously at the small link unit. "He wants to know why any worker will come to work when your Club is ready to supply all his needs for nothing."

"Maybe he won't," Adam paused soberly. "But that problem isn't entirely new. Automated machines are already producing most of our material necessities. Now—if we let them—they can supply everything."

"Is that good?" Joseph squirmed restively on the bench. "The senator wants to know who will buy anything—when everything is free. What will happen to capital? Dividends and profits? Free enterprise?"

His dark, pain-bitten face twitched with disturbed emotion; Adam thought he was about to cry.

"The senator wants to know how we can make a living."

"I suppose the social and economic structure is always based on technology," Adam said. "If contact brings us a new technology, we'll have to make social and economic adjustments. I wonder myself what they'll be."

He grinned into Joseph's woebegone countenance.

"At the worst, I guess the Monks can come around to accept the benefits of contact, like everybody else."

"But think of your Aunt Victoria." Joseph grimaced at the egg. "Think of her feelings. Her social position. Her pride. Imagine her begging handouts from a damned machine. She'd die first!"

"I think she'll come around," Adam said. "She's got more pluck than you know."

The rush of the jets was suddenly louder above.

"General Monk has something more to say." Joseph darted back to his feet. "He was at the shindy, and he'd caught your broadcasts. He doesn't like what he heard about handing out your damned gadgets to everybody. To children and criminals. To the race gangs right here in Westmark. He calls it a commie plot to liberate and arm and organize every enemy of our society."

Adam held up the contact unit.

"These aren't weapons," he protested. "They won't obey commands to attack or destroy. They can't be used to hurt anybody." He grinned ironically. "Passing them around isn't quite so bad as letting people buy mail-order rifles."

"But you intend to turn insane killers loose!" Joseph scowled

131

uneasily at the golden egg. "What happens when they run amuck?"

Adam hesitated, looking at the contact unit.

We can protect all who ask protection, its sourceless voice announced. *We can warn of danger. We can rotate a human body out of phase with a knife or a fist or a missile.*

Joseph flinched from it uneasily.

But such protection will seldom be required. Pathological killers are a symptom of the sickness in your society. They will disappear, as contact relieves the causes of crime. We suggest that your world is in far less danger from psychotic killers than it is from the selfish power groups who oppose contact.

"General Monk won't swallow that." Joseph tweaked at his pointed beard and blinked at the roaring jets. "Here's your message from him." His black eyes stabbed back at Adam. "You probably know he's the local *Man First* commander. He has been in touch with General Masters, our world commander."

"With Tom Jett, you mean," Adam said. "That was his name when the transgalactic team picked him up on the moon."

"Masters is on his way here now." Joseph scowled vindictively. "He is bringing weapons that he won't trust to anybody else. General Monk instructed me to tell you that if your machine is still here at noon, local time, Masters will attack it with weapons never seen on Earth."

"The machine can shield itself."

"Against our little bombs and missiles." Joseph nodded toward the crater Adam had passed. "But Masters was off the Earth long enough to pick up powers as far advanced as your machine."

Adam stood bleakly silent, thinking of the killer virus and the genifacts and the tripus. If *Man First* was vulnerable, he had failed to find where. Joseph saw his doubt.

"Can't you be reasonable, son?"

He flushed hotly, because he had never wanted Joseph to call him son.

"I used to think you were intelligent." The sweaty little

man hopped toward him like a nervous bird, but shied away from the egg. "Why won't you use your mind? Consider what this insane promise of everything for nothing will do to us. Not just to the Monks and Kayren—if she still means anything to you. But to men in general. If you make everything free, you'll kill all incentive. You'll take the meaning out of life."

"I don't think so," Adam protested quickly. "Life offers goals enough, beyond the physical things the machine can supply. Myself, I want to learn what the machine can teach me about the transgalactic culture. That should take a few years! Then I might take up science or sports or art or space exploration. More likely I'd work with the Club. Maybe I could even earn a membership. If life needs new meanings, we can invent them."

He weighed the egg in his hand.

"The trouble with you—with all the Monks—is that you want to look at most men as means. Workers, consumers, voters, soldiers—meat machines to be manipulated by the few in power. But our new freedoms can give each person an importance of his own."

"But is he worth it?" Joseph shrugged disdainfully. "Has the average man the brain and principle and taste to use all the gifts you want to bestow? You're throwing pearls to swine!"

"An old argument," Adam said. "In fact, we've debated it before. You're the classicist. You and the bishop claim that men are born corrupt. You feel that all goodness has to be taught and enforced by society."

"If goodness exists at all." Joseph nodded sardonically.

"But the transgalactic culture takes a more romantic stand," Adam said. "It values the individual above society. The romanticist believes that we are born with a fund of natural goodness—which may be destroyed by a bad society. To the contact machine, I'm afraid you and the bishop and the senator and the general look like instruments of a very bad society."

"I'd call myself a sane conservative." Joseph squinted fearfully down at his watch and fearfully up at the roaring sky.

"But we've no time to talk politics. Don't forget that General Masters will attack at noon—unless you have removed that machine."

"We won't remove it." Frowning at the golden egg, Adam groped frantically for a way of getting through to Joseph. "But look around this park!" he whispered desperately. "You've seen the slums. The hungry children crying in the stinking hallways. The gangs and the garbage in the streets. The pinching want. The killing ignorance. The suffocating tyranny of landlords and loan sharks and brutal cops and crooked labor bosses and dirty politicians—like the senator! These people need the freedoms we offer—"

"I'd call you a lunatic liberal—but it's past eleven! I've got to go." His brown hatchet face twitching as if with mingled emotions, Joseph reached out to shake hands. "I'm disappointed, Adam. I'd hoped to find more sense in you. I—I don't know what to tell poor Mary—"

His ragged voice trailed away.

"On second thought—" His eyes fixed on the golden egg. "On second thought, I'll take that damned gadget with me." His gaunt claw wavered, retreated timidly, snatched the egg. "I think the generals will want to see it."

He scurried away with it, and turned briefly back.

"Goodbye, Adam. I'll have to tell your mother you've let the family down."

With a backward glance at the drumming sky, he scuttled away through the smog-burnt trees. Adam watched him out of sight, and then turned heavily back toward the contact machine.

The mist-filled moat was already wider around it. Those luminous plumes were still dissolving rock and raising graceful walls of mint-new metal and gem-bright crystal. Awed at the swift precision of their work, he stopped for a moment to stare.

But he had failed. If *Man First* had any secret weakness, he had not found it. These ultimate wonders of automated technology were all for nothing. He had not convinced Joseph; the Club could not fight; Tom Jett was going to attack at noon. The Monks would inherit the Earth.

He shrugged and plodded ahead. He stumbled through the rubble around the missile crater and climbed the ramp the machine had made for him across its coldly glowing excavation. He reached a tall arch of sapphire crystal, erected since he came out.

Stop, Commander Cave!

The machine's keen voice came from nowhere, with overtones of Polly Ming.

We must warn you that your life is in danger if you return to the machine. A hostile human being has entered in your absence. She comes armed with illicit weapons from outside the Earth. She is waiting to kill you.

IX

THE SWEET VOICE of the machine hit him through the humid heat like a snowball in his face. He stumbled back from the luminous gloom beyond the sapphire arch, trying to get hold of himself. He had not been prepared for this.

Breathless under the broiling sun, he caught the bright new railing. The hot metal stung his hands. He let it go and stood gasping, peering through the glare at the cratered park and the sandbagged roofs around it and the jets shrieking across the smog-stained sky.

It was all too much. He had reached no truce with the Monks, found no move against *Man First*. In less than an hour, the attack would hit the contact machine. This killer waiting inside it was a pointless insult on top of defeat—

Or was it reason for hope?

Could it be another hint, like Joseph Runescribe's truce mission, of some unseen weakness in *Man First?* He saw no clue to the nature of the weakness—if it did exist at all— but the bare possibility caught his breath and spun him back to face the sapphire arch.

"She?" he called. "Who is she?"

The assassin is a female human being, the machine's noise-less voice answered instantly. *But she is shielded from our sensors by a technology as sophisticated as our own. We are unable to determine her identity.*

"How did she get inside?"

The same way Solomon Smith reached the Man First cell to rescue you. She is using a device which rotates her particles of mass to interpenetrate our own.

"Why does she want to kill me?"

Her personal motives are uncertain, but she is acting for Man First. The conditions of contact require that we have a human commander. Your death would force us to withdraw from Earth at once.

He hesitated, glancing back into the brassy glare of June.

"How is she armed?"

Her weapons are concealed from us.

"Where is she now?"

Her exact location is still indeterminate. She is waiting out of phase with our mass. She can emerge into phase at any point inside or near the machine.

In the stifling heat, he shivered.

"Can you—can you give me a weapon?"

The conditions of contact allow us to bring no weapons to Earth. We can supply you another link unit, but that cannot be used in any way for violence.

He dug instinctively into his pockets, and found not even a penknife. Searching wildly for any kind of weapon, he ran back to the nearest crater and twisted a wrought-iron bar from a shattered bench. Marching back up the ramp, he met a massive metal grille raised against him in the archway.

"Open up!" he shouted. "I'm coming back aboard."

The grille stayed shut.

We cannot allow you to carry any weapon into the machine. The conditions of contact strictly forbid us to support any sort of armed conflict.

Angrily, he hammered on the grille.

"If I'm in command, I order you to open up."

You cannot contravene the conditions. In any case, a mere club would be useless against the waiting killer.

"Then I'll go in without it." He tossed the iron club into the glowing moat. "Open the way."

We cannot shield you inside the machine. We advise you not to enter.

"I am in command," he shouted defiantly. "I come unarmed. I intend no violation of the conditions of contact. I order you to let me in."

After a long half-second, the grille divided. The two halves slid deliberately aside. Breathing hard, he strode through the arch into a curved and sloping corridor. Something chimed softly, and the pale ghost of a golden egg floated in front of him.

Your new contact unit, the machine said. *You may need it.*

He reached for the floating shadow. Something whined like an empty mosquito, and he felt the link unit become hard and sleek and warmly real in his fingers.

You are entering against our advice. Now we advise you to take refuge in your chambers. We cannot shield you anywhere, but we will have an instant's warning of any intrusion there.

"I didn't know I had chambers," he said. "Show me the way there."

Follow the corridor.

He followed the corridor, clutching the egg. He was listening for the sound of danger, but all he heard was the pad of his own footsteps and the harsh rasp of his own breathing. The machine itself seemed queerly still.

"Show me everything you can," he commanded. "If I have to defend myself with empty hands, at least I want to know what's around me. Show me the spaces where a human being could hide."

The killer is waiting out of phase, the machine reminded him. *Not in normal space.*

"Anyhow, I want to see the whole machine."

When he reached the elevator at the end of the corridor, the walls of cage and shaft had become transparent. Rising slowly, he looked out into the working parts of the contact machine.

The view dismayed him. Though he had not hoped to penetrate many billion years of technology at one glance, he had expected something he could grasp, some familiar ground on which he could plan to meet the killer. But he found nothing that let him feel at home.

Though he saw shape and color and motion, there was no part of the machine that he could recognize as wheel or piston, pipe or valve, motor or solenoid, switch or transistor or anything else.

The contact team had been grossly unfair to put him in command of the machine, he reflected bitterly. It was like pushing a Stone Age savage into a modern automated factory. He saw nothing useful. No vacant space where he could hope to hide. No strategic niche where his back might be protected. No object that he could snatch for a weapon.

"Enough," he muttered. "Let's get on to the chambers."

The walls turned opaque again, and he stepped out of the elevator into a tiny room that did invite him to feel at home. The lamp and the reclining chair and the shelf of well-thumbed books belonged to Earth. The inspector's dazzling color photograph on the wall was signed, *From Polly, with love.* But not with love to him. The half bottle of Mexican tequila sitting beside two blue glasses reminded him that the machine had come to him from Solomon Smith.

He sloshed reeking tequila into a glass and raised it ironically toward Polly's picture—

The killer! The machine's silent voice struck like a stabbing blade. *Behind you!*

He whirled and gasped and dropped the drink. He saw the killer—a misty ghost, growing swiftly real in the open doorway of the bath behind him. Barefoot, she wore little but a tight web of green-glowing wire. Holding something that looked like a dagger with a sharp blue flame for a blade, she came at him with a soundless rush.

"Kayren!" The recognition stunned him. "No! No!"

She raised her pale blue blade. Creased by the tight

138

wires of the glowing net, her face was a taut white mask, scarcely human. Her eyes were distended, all pupil, queerly glazed.

He snatched at her lifted wrist. His hand slipped through her flesh, as if it had been shadow. The dagger flashed down toward his body, looking brightly real. Perhaps her body was still out of phase with his, but he knew her weapon wasn't. He met it with the golden egg in his left hand.

Through the egg, he felt a jarring impact. The flame of the dagger exploded into blinding blue. A jolt of electricity numbed his arm. Egg and dagger clattered to the floor.

She recoiled from him, into a karate crouch. She was going to kick. That meant, he thought, that her body must come into phase with his, into his reach. And the glowing web must be what controlled her phase.

He crouched to meet her. When she kicked, he raked wildly at the strands that bit into her calf and ankle. Bright wires snapped. Green fire crackled. A hot bitter reek took his breath. Over all her body, the glowing wire turned black. With a moaning gasp, she crumpled to the floor.

Kneeling over her, he ripped off the brittle web, flung away the flat black case against her spine where the wires were rooted. Her glazed eyes had closed. Limp, breathing heavily, she made no response when he called her name and slapped her cheeks.

She shivered and relaxed again, as he gathered her up in his arms. He was about to carry her to the chair when he saw the wall dividing to reveal a bed. He placed her there and covered her with the sheet. He picked up the bottle of tequila, frowning at it doubtfully.

We can supply a less primitive medication, the machine said. *One that will neutralize the psychodrugs in her brain.*

The small golden egg rose like a tiny ship from the floor. Floating over a glass, it made a faint mosquito whine. A pale-blue fluid poured out, to fill the glass. Its heady odor tingled in his nostrils.

He carried the glass to Kayren. She whimpered protestingly when he moved her head, but with that wine-like scent in her face she gulped from the glass and lay back again, breathing more easily.

"Well?" He peered at the egg. "Did I violate the conditions?"

By no means, that sourceless voice assured him. *The Club is not concerned with merely human violence, but rather with the violent use of non-human artifacts such as those Man First has obtained.*

"She loved me, once." A delayed terror shook him. He stood numb and cold beside the bed, his voice a husky whisper. "Why did she come to kill me?"

Her mind had been manipulated. She is not responsible.

"But I saw her not a week ago." He stopped to stare at her sleeping face. "Just the day I got back from the moon. She looked all right then." He frowned at the bright little egg. "How did it happen?"

She can inform us. If she revives in time—

The piercing voice stopped abruptly. He felt a jolting vibration, heard a muffled rumbling. Kayren moved and whimpered on the bed.

Commander Cave! The mute voice was sharper, with fewer overtones of Polly Ming. *The opponents of contact are launching a heavy attack, without waiting for noon. They are preparing to use illicit weapons from outside. We may be forced to abandon the mission.*

"I am in command," he protested sharply. "I won't give up the mission."

We are bound by the conditions of contact, the machine reminded him. *We cannot engage in war.*

"But you can shield the machine."

From the weapons of Earth. But our opponents are bringing up outside weapons. Our shields may fail. In any case, the attack may endanger the people of Westmark. If that happens, the conditions of contact will require us to withdraw.

"Stand—stand fast!" He gulped at the tight, dry hoarseness in his throat. "Shield the machine as long as you can."

What can you gain by delay?

Desperately, he bent over Kayren. She was breathing evenly, deeply asleep. She whimpered faintly when he called her name.

"We must wake her," he said. "We must learn what she knows about the forces and intentions of *Man First*. Maybe she can tell us how to get our story through to the people of the world."

The time is short. We may be forced to leave at any instant.

"Kayren, wake up!" He seized her shoulders to shake her flaccid body. "Please wake up!"

She moaned faintly.

Kayren Hunter, you can wake up. The machine's silent voice turned more intense. *We are cleansing the psychodrugs from your body, to set you free again. You can wake up now. You can sit up. You can speak.*

Her eyes fluttered open, blankly staring. She sat up in the bed, which promptly tilted to fit her new position. She smiled vaguely at him.

"Hello, Adam." Her husky, slumber-dulled voice seemed pleased but not surprised. "So sleepy. Please don't mind."

"Please wake up!" he begged. "It's vital. Tell me who sent you here. Was it *Man First?*"

"Don't know." She yawned charmingly. "Don't remember."

You can remember now, the machine said. *We have set you free from Man First. We are sweeping the drugs from your brain. Now you can remember everything.*

Her bright head nodded. Still dilated, her dark eyes blinked at Adam. A languorous smile parted her lips.

"I remember now," she murmured softly. "I remember everything."

"Tell me." He tried not to shout. "Tell me about *Man First.*"

"What about *Man First?*" Vague trouble shadowed her face. "What do you want to know?"

"Everything!" He caught his breath and lowered his voice and tried to be specific. "Please Kayren. I already know about Thomas Jett. He was picked up on the moon by the transgalactic contact team, over twenty years ago. He came back with knowledge and weapons from outside. Using the name Jett Masters, he set up the secret group called *Man First*. He's fighting contact. Fighting progress. Fighting the non-white races on Earth. Actually, I suppose he's fighting for personal power. That much I know."

He leaned toward her dreamy face.

"Do you belong to *Man First?*"

"They say I do."

"Who says it?"

"The senator," she breathed sleepily. "General Monk. General Masters. They all told me to work for *Man First* and keep the secrets of *Man First*."

We have set you free, the machine said. *You can reveal the secrets now.*

"Tell me all about it," Adam begged. "How did you get into *Man First?* What do you know about it? What did Masters make you do?"

Her white body moved lazily, half uncovered.

Time is short. Speak quickly.

Her eyes moved without wonder to the bright golden egg in Adam's hand, and back to his face. Her smooth face warmed slowly, with the smile of a drowsy child.

"I like you, Adam. You were cruel when you broke our engagement, but I like you anyhow. I'll tell you everything."

The bed adjusted itself as she moved, becoming a kind of chair.

"The senator phoned me the day you left for the moon. He offered me my mother's old position. I thought he wanted to make up for the way you had left me, and of course I had no other plans. I took the job."

Eyelids sinking heavily, she seemed clearly rational yet queerly without feeling for anything she said. It was almost, he thought, as if she were relating a meaningless dream.

"I thought it would be just an office job, but the very day I came to work we flew in General Monk's space jet to a field somewhere in the woods—he said the location was secret."

"The *Man First* Headquarters," Adam whispered. "I was there."

"Queer creatures met us when we got off the jet. They looked like black men, till you saw they weren't human at all. I was shaking, but the senator spoke to them in a strange language and told me not to be afraid of them. He said they were genifacts."

Perhaps she had been frightened then, but her voice was serenely even now.

"The genifacts led me to an office building, and the senator introduced me to General Masters. A tall good-looking energetic man—with something in his eyes that petrified me. The senator said my real boss would be the general."

She sat floating in a drowned world, where even fear was dead.

"I felt terrified when the senator went out and left us together, yet somehow Masters fascinated me. He was smooth enough. He began to tell me about the job. It would be secret and exciting but not really dangerous. It paid well, and it would let me serve humanity.

"While we were talking in the office, one of the black genifacts brought cocktails. Mine had a queer taste—something like plastic cement." She made a face of faint distaste. "I was frightened. I told Masters I wouldn't take the job, and I got up to run after the senator."

The happy indolence of her smile, more than anything she said, was raising gooseflesh on him.

"Masters wouldn't let me go. He had two genifacts hold me down, while he poured the drink in my mouth. I spat it in his face. Then he sent for a kind of needle and gave me an injection."

Lazily relaxed, she stretched her body in the chair.

"That injection paralyzed me," she murmured dreamily. "I couldn't run away. I sat down and stood up when Masters told me to. He said I was now a member of *Man First*, fighting to protect the Earth from space invasion. He said I would obey his commands and then forget them. He said I would never tell *Man First* secrets to anybody else—"

"A monstrous thing!" Adam gasped out in spite of himself. "That must be what happened to me—if I really killed my father." Suddenly he clutched the little golden egg in both clammy hands. "Can't you help me remember—if I did kill my father!"

There is no time for such experiments, the machine replied. *We are now intercepting messages between General Monk and General Masters. General Monk is at his field headquarters outside the city. General Masters is now circling the park in a special military jet, carrying outside armament. If he attacks with that, we must abandon our mission.*

"I know that special jet." Her soft murmur came from a lotus land where all events were meaningless. "It's disguised to look familiar, but it came from space. It's the flyer that belongs to the tripus—"

"Huh!" Adam started. "What do you know about the tripus?"

Tell us quickly. This may be important.

"I saw the tripus in the swimming pool." She smiled mistily at Adam. "General Masters made me come with him. I had to do everything he said. At the swimming pool he told me to watch the tripus. Then he told one of his black genifacts to dive into the pool."

Though her voice was still dreamily serene, he saw bright beads of sweat along her lip.

"The tripus ate it." Her vague smile was fading. "Masters made me watch while it snapped the red pieces out of the water. Then he told me that if I ever disobeyed him, or spilled *Man First* secrets, he would feed me to the tripus."

She shivered slightly to some thin ghost of terror.

"Don't let it eat me," she whimpered huskily. "Adam, don't let it."

"We can keep you safe." Clutching her nerveless hand, he tried to quench a smoldering doubt of that. "If you'll just tell us all about it."

"I trust you, Adam." She smiled tenderly, as if an ugly dream had passed. "Who's afraid of the tripus?"

Quickly! Tell us the actions of the tripus.

"The senator and General Monk came out to the pool for a conference with it. It understands English, but it can't speak. Masters spoke to it from the edge of the pool with his feet in the water to show his trust. It reached out of the pool to write on a kind of blackboard."

She stretched again, with a drowsy yawn.

"The tripus knew General Monk, but not the senator. Masters introduced them. He had met the tripus somewhere on his travels with the contact team. It is a sea creature, but its home planet needs more water. It followed Masters back to Earth, to buy the Antarctic ice. It is going to pay with the weapons and secrets Masters wants for *Man First*."

Moving slowly, like a floating swimmer, she lifted a hand to touch Adam's face.

"The senator didn't like the deal. He was horrified about the eaten genifact, and he didn't want to trust the tripus. He was afraid it wouldn't be satisfied with just the ice. He thought it might want to drain the oceans, too."

She smiled as if to some pleasing dream.

"Masters got mad. He said he had already made promises that had to be kept. He said collapse of the *Man First* movement would let a colored revolution wipe out the white race. He said there was ice enough in Greenland, if the tripus wasn't satisfied with Antarctica."

Her tender fingers caressed his lips.

"Adam, you're so sweet. I'm glad you didn't let me kill you."

"Please tell me about the tripus."

Her full lips pouted prettily. "The senator finally agreed to go along. He agreed things had gone too far to stop, and he said he had played dirty pool before. Then they talked about my mission."

"What was your mission?"

"Masters taught me how to use that phase gear to slip through walls or anything. He gave me a sort of needle. He told me what to do. He sent me to do it, in that flyer with the tripus.

"The flyer came from nowhere. I saw it standing in the pool. It looked like a wingless jet, and it had the *Man*

145

First markings, but most of it was full of water. The tripus swam into it through an underwater lock. Masters sent me up a ramp, to a special air tank where I could breathe."

She was sunk deep in her drugged repose, her murmur so faint that he leaned to listen.

"The tripus took me somewhere. We were in a hotel— the flyer had what Masters called a mass phase drive, so that it could slide through things. The signal flashed, and I did my mission. I came out of the compartment in my phase gear with the needle, and slipped into a hotel room. A man was sleeping there. I shot an injection into his arm—"

"Wait!" Adam gasped. "Was that hotel on the moon?"

"I don't know." She shrugged lazily. "The tripus didn't talk to me. Masters didn't say."

"The gravity?" he whispered. "Did you feel lighter in the room?"

She nodded drowsily.

"I thought it was the phase gear, but something made me bouncy." Frowning distractedly, she touched her bright hair. "I had trouble walking, and bumped my head on the ceiling."

"Then you were on the moon!"

Adam lifted the golden egg on his palm.

"That hotel was the Tycho-Hilton," he shouted breathlessly. "The sleeping man was my father. That shot was the virus that killed him. But I didn't do it! My mind was not manipulated. I didn't kill my father—"

We must interrupt. Although Kayren Hunter is revealing violation of the conditions of contact which should not have been permitted, our time has run out. The disguised phase flyer overhead has launched a weapon and disappeared. The weapon is falling toward this spot. We must withdraw before it strikes.

"Not now!" He was hoarse and desperate. "Now we've got to stay. Shield the machine!"

You underestimate Man First. General Masters has secured sophisticated alien weapons. Although we cannot identify the device now falling, it has the mass of a thermonuclear bomb.

"Can't you shield us?" he shouted bitterly. "Don't your precious conditions require you to defend us?"

We must protect the city. That is why we must withdraw. Althought we can shield the machine itself from almost any weapon, we cannot defend the surrounding target area without a military effort that would violate the conditions of contact. The falling weapon is aimed at the machine. If we are gone, it will not be activated—

"I refuse to leave."

Then we must leave you.

A freezing panic shook his body.

"Wait!" He gasped for breath and tried to put the panic down. "In spite of this attack, I think the *Man First* tactics show some secret weakness. I think the general is somehow bluffing. I'm going to call his hand. That's the only chance I see."

We can discover nothing vulnerable about Man First. We compute a nine-to-one probability that the falling weapon exceeds your greatest thermonuclear bomb in radius of total destruction. We advise you strongly to let us remove you.

"Take Kayren." He bent to brush her lips with his. "Keep her safe—"

Her bare arms caught him, softly clung.

"Keep me, Adam! Keep me with you."

You are both unwise. Your lives will be in gravest danger. But we can wait no longer. The alien weapon is only sixty seconds overhead—

The machine stopped for half a precious second.

Adam Cave, we have a personal message for you. From the contact inspector.

Still soundless, the voice changed.

"Please, Adam!" It was Polly Ming. "Please don't risk your lives for nothing—"

"It's not for nothing, Polly! Can't you help?"

"We have done all we can. Kayren Hunter's evidence might have been used against *Man First*, but it came too late. Any action from our team, at this point, might detonate that falling weapon."

"What can I do?"

"Nothing, Adam. We have simply met too many Monks. You know the conditions of contact. Your people have the freedom of choice. To our regret, it seems they have chosen no contact. Your refusal to leave the target position is therefore childish—"

"Anyhow, I'm staying."

"To an unwise idealist, we send our love—"

The noiseless voice was cut off. The contact machine was abruptly gone. Blind in the sudden brazen glare, gasping in the hot smog, he found himself outside in the park. Kayren clung to him, whimpering like a child. The roar of the *Man First* attack broke over them, the boom and rattle and deathly yell. Squinting up into the blazing haze, he found the falling weapon.

X

HE TURNED TO RUN and found the crater. The machine had left them where it stood, but that point was now a flat peak, ringed with the deep crater where mass had been dug for the crystal tower. The ramp across it was gone.

Swaying back from that chasm, he blinked again into the smoky sky. The alien weapon was a finned metal cylinder. Low, now, it sloped toward the peak, a blurred rotor whirling behind it. He flinched from a sudden ugly screech and hammer, saw quick black perforations stitched across it, saw the rotor crumple.

It tumbled toward them, crippled death.

He snatched Kayren into his arms, staggered across the tiny mesa, stumbled into the first shallow pit the machine had dug for its own foundation. He crouched there, arching his body to cover her, his face tucked against his arms. He heard it hit.

A slapping crash of crumpling metal. For an instant of agony, he held his breath. But there was no blaze of hell, no smash of blackness, no hail of debris. It had not been activated—or had the *Man First* gunners shot down their own weapon?

"Keep me, Adam!" Kayren clung to him dreamily. "Keep me always."

Cautiously, he raised his head. The little pit was fringed with grass and broken shrubs and one undamaged yellow dandelion. The finned cylinder lay punctured and flattened beneath its twisted rotor. All around, the new peak sloped steeply down into the ring-shaped trench the machine had cut with its jets of silent fire.

Whee-whamp!

He ducked from the howl and thump of a rocket that left its drifting plume where the golden dome had stood and burst behind him on the road where he had talked to Joseph Runescribe.

Monk Park was now a lurid battlefield, plowed to raw, red chaos. North and west and south, the old apartment houses loomed dimly from a gray sea of smoke, half of them shattered or burning. He crouched again from a row of battle-painted tanks that came grinding out of the haze, pumping projectiles into the space above his head where the contact machine had been. They reached the crater rim, ceased fire, whirled away into the smoke. Bitterly, still bent low, he shook his fist toward the gray granite cube of the Monk Building, which loomed unharmed among the downtown skyscrapers in the smoky east.

"Okay, Senator!" He spat into the choking smoke. "I hope this is what you want—when we could have had all the best of a billion worlds and a billion years of progress. I hope you like it, Senator Monk!"

"He's not so bad," Kayren's drowsy voice protested, as serenely sweet as if everything had been a fleeting dream. "The others didn't trust him. That's why they sent me back to his office after my mission was done. They wanted me to watch him—but what was that?"

He saw her listening. In the relative hush, since the firing had subsided, he heard a human cry from the battered cylinder. It came again through a red-handled oval door, which hung jolted half open by the crash.

"Christ!" The broken tones were dimly familiar. "Help me—"

"That's no weapon," he whispered to Kayren. "An escape capsule! Wait for me here."

He motioned her back into the pit. Crouching, he scrambled over the peak to the crumpled vehicle. Glistening in the sun beside it, where he and Kayren had first stood, he saw that little golden link unit. The machine must have dropped it with them, but now it was an ironic mockery of his splendid dreams of contact. He kicked it bitterly aside.

"Hello," he called. "Who are you?"

"Dying—" came that agonized moan. "Get me out of here!"

He wrenched the twisted door aside, loosened the straps, lifted out the injured man. The blood-sodden flying suit bore five silver stars and a *Man First* patch. He turned the loose head and recognized the cragged, fleshless face.

"Jett!" he gasped. "I thought you were attacking."

At sight of him, the ice-blue eyes dulled and set. All that mad, hard, vital charisma flowed out of Jett like his own thick blood. He lay crumpled like a spaceman doll with the stuffing gone, empty, ugly.

"Was." Spasms of pain punctuated the rasping whisper. "All over now. All wrong for us. Partner—stinking coward —lost his nerve. Ditched me. Ditched me to die." The froth-rimmed lips twitched viciously. "Stinking yellow rat. E-jected me into the battle. Intending my own men to kill me!"

Adam stared. "What's all this?"

Jett breathed painfully.

"Your damn doing." The cold eyes glared. "You and

your girl. We thought she was safe. But they got to her. Mucking contact team. Picked her mind for evidence."

His sneering lips spat blood.

"Violation—violation of their damn conditions of contact. Mucking inspector acted on her evidence. Tried to arrest the tripus. Stinking yellow bug! Lost his nerve. Ditched me here to go to hell. Scuttled into space."

The glazing eyes fluttered shut.

"Damn—damn genifacts." The angry force was dying from his papery voice. "I made 'em. Counted on 'em. To watch the tripus. At the showdown—took his orders. Helped pitch me out."

He quivered and stiffened, bubbling as he breathed.

Adam looked up at the shattered ruin that rimmed the park. He shook his head blackly, groping for the final significance of those pain-broken words. A sniper's bullet ricocheted and screamed away, somewhere in the drifting smoke.

"Well, Cave."

Ducking from the bullet's whine, he found Jett's eyes on him again, now open wide and oddly calm.

"You've got plenty to forgive." Jett dribbled red. "I'm your enemy. Fought you. Took your girl. Sent her to kill your father. But now I'm bleeding to death."

Jett rattled and bubbled, yet his eyes remained coldly alert, opaquely flat, no more human, Adam thought, than the eyes of the tripus had been.

"What about it, Cave?"

Black hate clenched his fists and set his jaw and chilled his sweaty body. He wanted to smash Jett's narrow, black-browed face and toss him off the peak to die. Weakness seized him. He couldn't breathe. His whole body shook.

"Well?" The red-spattered lips made no sound. "What about it?"

A bullet slapped the flattened capsule and buzzed away into the smoke. A pebble clattered behind him. Startled, he twisted and saw Kayren. She had climbed out of the little pit. She came walking over the summit, half clad in the sheet from the machine, smiling dreamily.

"Get down!" he shouted hoarsely. "Please get down."

She came on instead. He pulled her down beside him. When she saw Jett, her dream turned to nightmare. She crouched back against him. He felt her shudder, saw her eyes dilate.

"No! No! No!" She covered her face with bloodless hands. "I told about *Man First*. Now he'll feed me to the tripus!"

"He can't hurt you now," he whispered. "His own men shot him down."

"Right, Cave," Jett sighed. "Your move now."

His own spasm of hatred had passed. He opened the punctured space jacket, ripped off the clotted cloth, found the leaky black slit in the gaunt rib cage.

"Sorry, Jett," he muttered. "Nothing I can do."

We can save his life.

The noiseless voice drew his eyes to the golden contact unit. Kayren had picked it up. She held it in both white hands, staring at it sleepily.

He must ask for contact. He must promise to observe the conditions established by the Club. He must agree to cooperate with the transgalactic contact team, and to dissolve the Man First organization, and to bear witness against the captured tripus.

"Well, Jett?" Adam grinned at him. "What about it?"

His lusterless eyes stared at nothing. A fly crawled across his rigid face and settled on the wound. His red-caked lips twitched faintly, shaping soundless words.

"I—I promise."

Accept the link unit. Take it in your hands.

His black-haired hands fumbled feebly, and Kayren folded them over the golden egg. Adam heard a thin mosquito hum, saw a misty tendril, barely visible, reaching from the egg to probe the bullet slit.

The rictus of agony was smoothed from Jett's gray face. The thick blood stopped welling from the wound. He drew a long, untroubled breath, as if peacefully asleep. Kayren brushed the fly away.

Adam stood trembling in a great flood of illogical joy. Little as he owed Jett, his throat was aching and his eyes burned with tears. He reached out blindly for Kayren and touched her sleek shoulder.

"Oh!" She drew back quickly. "Adam, I'm naked."

Abruptly wide awake, washed all over with a pink embarrassment, she hastily pulled the inadequate sheet up around her.

"It's a little late for modesty." He stood grinning. "You came at me in the machine with nothing much except that dagger."

"Can you forgive me, Adam?" She turned pinker. "Even—even for your father?"

Sobering, he shrugged.

"Why not?" He frowned down at Jett. "If we forgive him." He put his arms around her. "How about forgiving me? I've been—" His voice caught. "I've been unfair to you, Kay. Sometime I'll tell you why."

He gazed into the gray smoke, thinking of Polly Ming and the engineer, shivering again to that old memory of his mother in Joseph's arms, forgotten since he was three.

"I guess I never really trusted you." He looked back into her breathless face. "I know I hurt you, calling off the wedding—"

Abruptly she gasped and whirled and clutched the sheet around her. Turning, he saw that the smoke was lifting. He saw people streaming across the raw missile pits from north and west and south. Leading them, waving bright little golden eggs, he began to recognize his father's disciples from the *caserío*.

"What are they saying?" Kayren bent her shining head to listen. "Can you hear?"

"*Viva!*" Pedro and Chino came to the brink of the trench, the red-haired Jaliscan between them. Their lifted link units burned in the blaze of noon. Their vibrant glad voices drifted across the pit. "*Viva el Contactor!*"

He stood up to stare. The teeming crowd was swelling. People poured out of the scarred apartment towers. People flowed from a new jam of cars on River Road. Uniformed men tumbled out of armored vehicles and ran shouting toward the crater.

"He's alive!" A dazzled joy lit Kayren's eyes. "They're saying your father is alive."

"He can't be." A dark pain blotted out his own quick spark of jubilation. "We all saw him dead."

"Skin me!"

Adam blinked and shook his head, reluctant to believe he had really heard that lazy, nasal drawl.

"Wake up, Cave. Contact has come."

Turning dazedly, he saw the stubby little landing craft floating beside the summit. The bubble had opened. Solomon Smith jumped off and gripped his hand.

"Good job with Jett." He staggered a little, breath reeking with tequila. "You and Kayren saved the whole operation."

"My father—" Anxious emotion caught Adam's voice. "He's really alive?"

"A transgalactic miracle!" Awe glinted in Smith's greenish eyes. "He was dead enough when we took him back to the team. Clinically dead. But the thing they call the engineer is a skinnish good biologist."

"The engineer?" He shivered again.

"He got the answer to that hairy virus. Another created virus, built out of your father's own genes. It multiplied in his body, absorbing the virus that had killed him, repairing each dying cell.

"James Cave was resurrected."

Resurrected? He stared blankly into Smith's raw-boned, one-sided grin, trying to understand what contact meant. He felt like a Stone Age savage on a jungle island, if a rocket had landed with books and television, tools and seeds, medicines and teachers—

No, it meant more than that. He felt afraid, even sad. The team had brought ten billion years of progress. More new things than he could hope to grasp. His old familiar world had ended. Earth would never be the same again.

"Where is he?" His shaking fingers caught the sleeve of Smith's grease-blotted coveralls. "Where is my father now?"

"He'll be along in the machine." Smith was bending over

Jett. "He'll set it back on the same foundation. We'll have to get out of his way."

He felt a dim, confused gratitude for people, noise, activity. Later, he could face the facts of contact. He could explore the new world dawning. Just now, he felt glad to be distracted.

Still sleeping, Jett gave no sign of awareness or pain when they lifted him to the deck of the landing craft. They laid him down carefully, the bright egg still gripped in both red hands.

"Adam!" Polly Ming called from the bubble as he stood up, and now her clear, gentle voice seemed to echo the soundless precision of the contact machine. "You have done well here. I want to thank you, for the team."

Stunning in something sleek and bright and violet, she glided out to meet him, flowed into his arms, raised her piquant face for him to kiss. Giddy with her enchantment, he heard Kayren gasp. He introduced them breathlessly.

"Kayren, this is the inspector. Chief of the transgalactic team. We call her Polly Ming. She comes from the Clouds of Magellan. She isn't human, but she was chosen for her high quotient of appeal."

Polly was demurely bewitching. Kayren shook hands with her, cooing too sweetly, then made a savage face at him.

"I'm human, Buster," her hot whisper hissed. "Just wait till you find out."

The landing craft ferried them out of the crater, to meet his father's excited disciples. Pedro and Chino and Jesus Sabio came scrambling aboard to shake his hand. He jumped off to greet O'Toole and the Turk. Their voices were drowned in a new wave of cheering.

Looking back, he saw the ghostly outline of the contact machine, the great dome swelling above the half-completed tower, so faint at first that he could see the gray granite cube of the Monk building against the smoky sky beyond it. Abruptly it was real, golden blaze and sapphire glow, in phase with Earth again, where it had stood before.

"*Viva!*" Pedro screamed. "*Viva el Salvador!*"

The cheering crowd pushed them forward. The wild

shouting rose again, and at last he saw his father. Bright of face, bright of eyes, bright of flowing hair, James Cave—no longer Jason Caine—came bounding down the ramp to meet the multitude.

The black Swan followed and, gravely radiant, she joined his father at the end of the ramp, above the busy plumes that once more filled the pit. Hushed and eager people streamed around them. Working side by side, they pressed a bright link unit into each seeking hand.

Adam stared, trying to feel the meaning of it. Each bright egg, for one individual, was a private line to the transgalactic culture. It was a wonderbox that many a billion years and many billion worlds had filled. It was freedom from need, from ignorance, from all oppression—

"—go along with Huxley." The fussy whine of Joseph Runescribe lifted out of the mob behind him. "A utopian society might be wonderful for robots, assembled in automated factories and untouched by human emotions. But we imperfect human beings would be perfectly miserable in any perfect world."

"Hogwash, Joseph!" The senator's blunt voice oozed unquenchable assurance. "You and the generals have your eyeballs where your something else ought to be. You want to kill the goose that's about to lay the golden egg."

"I never liked progress," Joseph droned. "If this ridiculous handout is progress, I don't like it now. If this transgalactic culture is the culture of science, give me the Stone Age. This insane utopian invasion will level every value in our own human culture back to zero."

"You take the Stone Age!" The senator snorted like a startled horse. "I'll help myself. I'm a Monk, and not for nothing. I plan to get myself into this transgalactic Club. You know—" A new idea checked his voice. "You know, I'd like to rewrite their holy canons of contact!"

"Why, Senator Saul!" Joseph was shocked.

"Why not?" the senator bugled. "Contact can't do much to human nature. Politics always was a poker game. This brave new world is just a game, the way I see it, with fatter jackpots piling up. I intend to learn to bluff the best of 'em. Man or monster!"

"I guess you've got the gall to do it." Joseph's voice sank back into his old urbane despair. "But, in my philosophy, change is always bad. Progress rots tradition. Talk about your billion years of progress on a billion planets! I'd trade all progress for a single afternoon in the agora of classical Athens."

A little Negro urchin slipped back between them, naked and grimy to the waist, eyes wide with pride, both grubby hands clutching his own golden egg. He sat on the ground behind an overturned park bench and began a quiet dialogue with the contact unit.

Presently it whined like a far-off mosquito. Applying the devices of its high technology to transform available mass, it extended a faintly glowing tendril to give him a double-dip peppermint ice cream cone.

"Adam!" His father's eyes had found him. "My son!"

James Cave sprang down from the ramp. The crowd parted, and he came striding to where Adam stood. He looked young, sound again, radiant. The black Swan watched from the ramp, her face aglow with devotion.

He was about to shake hands, but his father seized him in a hug that took his breath. Blinking at his tears of gladness, he presented Kayren and said they were going to be married.

His father kissed her heartily—and noticed her pink confusion. If the nudity taboo still embarrassed her, he said, the machine was now ready to supply any material need. He sent her up the ramp with the black Swan for a new outfit.

"You're going to have a busy honeymoon." His bright eyes smiled on Adam, gladly grave. "We've got a new world to make. Though the machine can give us nearly anything material, or any information, we are still responsible. We must see to it that our new world is better than the old."

He glanced impatiently back at the crystal tower rising around the machine.

"We'll soon have new machines coming out of this first center, to open contact all over the Earth. Will you take one of them to Hyderabad?"

He nodded willingly.

"Your old friend Kalinin will take the next to Novosibirsk—"

A thousand anxious hands were reaching for contact. He left his father handing out the golden links, and followed Kayren up into the shimmering tower. He knew that the unknown paths of change would hold surprise and peril and pain, but he felt ready to meet them now.

"I don't like it, Saul!" Joseph Runescribe's waspish whine rose out of the crowd. "This nightmare machine. This insane plague of unearned power. It's about to set the wrong people free. Look at that filthy brat!"

His narrow nose lifted at the Negro urchin sitting behind the broken bench, clutching his precious egg and licking up the last of his instant ice cream cone.

"What good will ten billion years of transgalactic culture do him, without some use of social force? Who will teach him his place in the world? Who will make him keep it?" A gathering terror quavered in his voice. "What will he do to us? He—and all the billions like him!"

The senator made an untroubled shrug, and they turned to stare at the Negro boy. Still absorbed in his dialogue with the contact unit, the child reached eagerly for a mint-new geometric puzzle it had made for him.

Parts of the puzzle looked like polished quartz. Parts of it were sparkling mist. As the boy began to work with it, queer symbols glowed and vanished inside the crystal parts. The golden egg hummed faintly in his lap; now and then his bent head nodded to its soundless voice. His lips moved, shaping names for those magic symbols. His face lit with dawning wonder. Presently his small body began to flicker into shadow and turn real again, as he learned to shift himself out of phase with Earth. He looked up and saw the staring men and shivered to the thrill of his perilous new freedom from them and from all coercion.

If you want to keep up with the best science fiction stories of the year, you will want to get your copy of:

WORLD'S BEST SCIENCE FICTION

1967

Selected and Edited by

Donald A. Wollheim and Terry Carr

Outstanding stories and novelettes from the science fiction and fantasy magazines of the world, including great tales by Roger Zelazny, Brian W. Aldiss, Frederik Pohl, Philip K. Dick, Avram Davidson, Michael Moorcock, and others.

"Entertaining and imaginative"
    —*Publishers Weekly*

Ace Book A-10   75¢

Ace Books, Inc. (Dept. MM)
1120 Avenue of the Americas
New York, N.Y. 10036